SPÉCIALITÉ **PREMIÈRE ET TERMINALE**

STUDYBAC

ANGLAIS, MONDE CONTEMPORAIN (LLCER)

AUTEUR
Professeur d'anglais en lycée et membre de jury en BTS,
Isabelle ARNAUD
est également formatrice en didactique des langues au Centre national de formation de l'enseignement technique et professionnel.

Studyrama

STUDYBAC

Des cahiers innovants pour apprendre en s'amusant !

Conformes aux programmes du nouveau Bac, ces cahiers ont été conçus par des professeurs sensibles à une méthode d'apprentissage issue de la pédagogie positive.

Ils comprennent l'essentiel à connaître, et proposent de nombreux jeux et exercices, ainsi que des cartes mentales ou des synthèses visuelles propices à la stimulation, la motivation et la concentration.

À vous de jouer !

Tronc commun

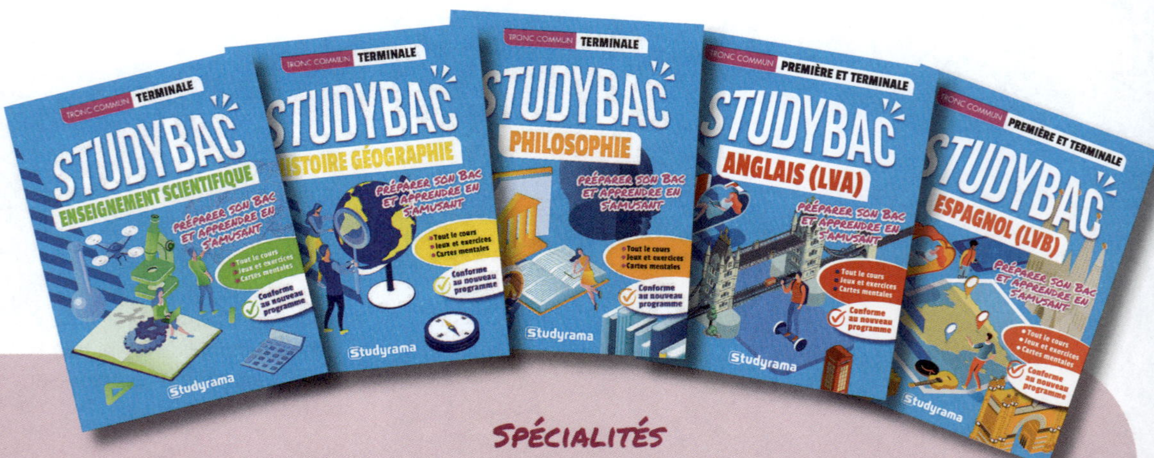

Spécialités

- Sciences économiques et sociales, Terminale
- Histoire-géographie, géopolitique et sciences politiques, Terminale
- Physique-chimie, Terminale
- Mathématiques, Terminale
- Sciences de la vie et de la Terre, Terminale
- Humanités, littérature et philosophie, Terminale

Sommaire

À FAIRE

Objectifs du jour Date : ....

1 ☐ Fait
2 ☐ Fait
3 ☐ Fait

NOTES

Objectifs du jour Date : ....

1 ☐ Fait
2 ☐ Fait
3 ☐ Fait

NOTES

Objectifs du jour Date : ....

1 ☐ Fait
2 ☐ Fait
3 ☐ Fait

NOTES

Objectifs du jour Date : ....

1 ☐ Fait
2 ☐ Fait
3 ☐ Fait

NOTES

À FAIRE

Objectifs du jour Date : ....

1

☐ Fait

2

☐ Fait

3

☐ Fait

NOTES

Objectifs du jour Date : ....

1

☐ Fait

2

☐ Fait

3

☐ Fait

NOTES

Objectifs du jour Date : ....

1

☐ Fait

2

☐ Fait

3

☐ Fait

NOTES

Objectifs du jour Date : ....

1

☐ Fait

2

☐ Fait

3

☐ Fait

NOTES

Auditive, kinesthésique ou visuelle : quel est votre type de mémoire ?

Pour bien vous connaître, voici un petit test à réaliser pour comprendre comment fonctionne votre mémoire.

Pour vous concentrer, vous avez tendance à :

- fermer les yeux .... ■
- mâchouiller votre stylo .... ▲
- vous boucher les oreilles .... ●

Pour réviser, vous avez besoin de :

- réécrire l'essentiel sur des fiches .... ▲
- réciter votre cours à haute voix .... ●
- relire vos notes encore et encore .... ■

Quand vous travaillez, vous êtes :

- si concentré(e) que vous en oubliez le monde qui vous entoure .... ●
- obligé(e) d'être dans un endroit familier .... ▲
- facilement déconcentré(e) par ce qui se passe autour .... ■

En cours, vous êtes plutôt du genre à :

- regarder le tableau ou la fenêtre .... ■
- écouter le professeur ou vos camarades .... ●
- vous balancer sur votre chaise .... ▲

Pour apprendre l'anglais, vous préférez :

- voyager dans un pays anglophone .... ▲
- lire des livres dans cette langue .... ■
- regarder des films en VO ou écouter des chansons .... ●

CALCULEZ VOTRE RÉSULTAT !

Vous avez + de ▲

votre mémoire est surtout
kinesthésique

Conseil : Faites et refaites les exercices de ce cahier. Les rappels de cours et les synthèses graphiques vous aideront à les réussir haut la main. Vous aimez le concret et les expériences. Vous vous rappelez plus facilement ce que vous avez vécu. Vous êtes sensible aux émotions et aux sensations, et avez besoin de vivre les choses. Votre stylo au capuchon mâchouillé, votre crayon de toujours et votre gomme seront vos meilleurs compagnons de bataille !

Vous avez + de ■

votre mémoire est surtout
visuelle

Conseil : Concentrez-vous sur les cartes mentales et autres synthèses graphiques, mais n'en oubliez pas le reste pour autant. Ce cahier richement illustré vous sera d'une grande aide.
Vous aimez les couleurs et les schémas. Vous vous rappelez plus facilement de ce que vous avez vu. Vous êtes à l'aise avec les détails, mais il vous faut associer les idées à des images. Votre stylo quatre couleurs et vos surligneurs seront vos armes les plus efficaces !

Vous avez + de ●

votre mémoire est surtout
auditive

Conseil : Récitez l'essentiel du cours et faites un maximum de choses à voix haute, y compris les exercices. Ceux incluant une vidéo seront particulièrement adaptés pour vous. Vous aimez les sons et le bruit. Vous vous rappelez plus facilement de ce que vous avez entendu. Vous retenez surtout les idées principales, il vous faut ainsi les trier et les écouter pour qu'elles restent gravées en vous. Votre voix, un enregistreur vocal et vos écouteurs seront vos plus précieux alliés !

☑ Première

☐ Terminale

Knowledge, creation, innovation

Savoirs, création, innovation

- **Production and circulation of knowledge**
  Production et circulation des savoirs
- **Sciences and technologies, promises and challenges**
  Sciences et techniques, promesses et défis

Production and circulation of knowledge

Production et circulation des savoirs

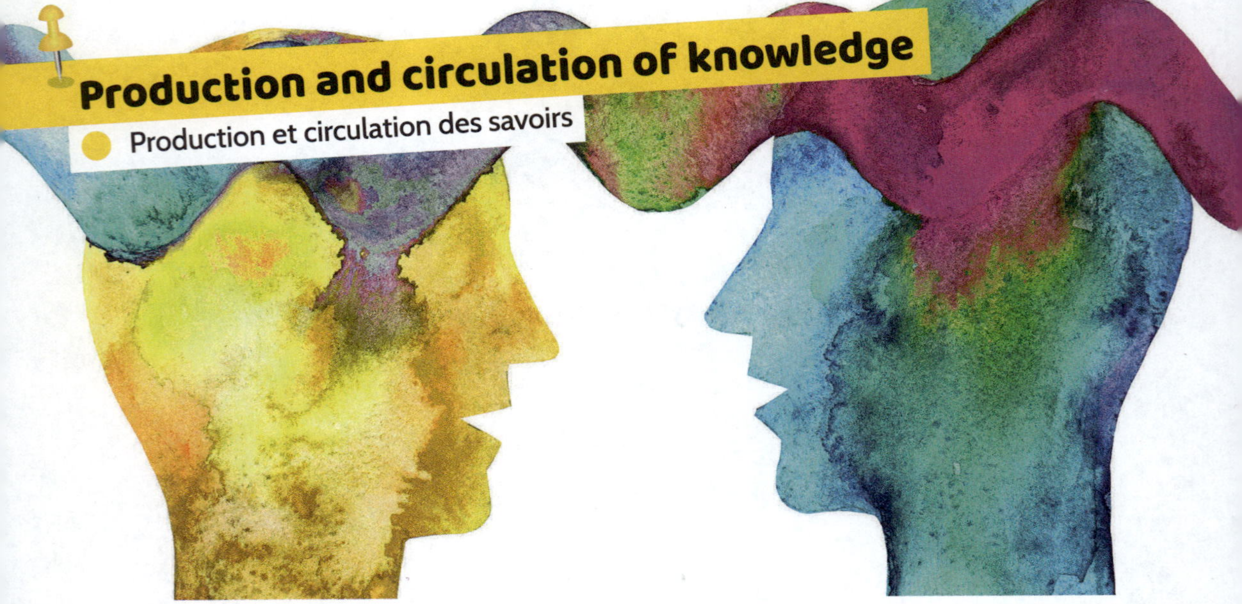

Knowledge society

An understanding of **knowledge** production begins with a broad network of knowledge producers, i.e. schools and universities such as Oxford and Cambridge in the United Kingdom or the Ivy league (Yale, Princeton, Harvard), the MIT (Massachusetts Institute of Technology), Stanford in the United States of America; and with all forms of education – whether on basic researches or on more applied types of researches associated especially with industry. They build, transmit and develop the knowledge and experience which are the sources of innovation. Knowledge **dissemination** **enables** individuals and companies to develop sciences and technologies. This is how a knowledge society is continuously **renewing itself**, by investing in education and **training**. It generates knowledge, shares it and makes information available to all members. Moreover, it is subject to a variety of comments, viewpoints, interpretations and applications.

The digital world

The digital world has become the new power source of education and knowledge, through constant connectivity and exchange of information. Content is generated by institutions, professionals and users in various forms: podcasts, blogs, online encyclopedias, **crowdsourcing** platforms.
Digitization is profoundly changing our cultural experience in terms of participation and individual or collective creation. Not only have digital technologies influenced **heritage** management and understanding, but they have also affected language, **mindset**, societies, and the way we identify with one another and form communities.
Unfortunately, the current digital divide stratifying the United States appears more transparent than segregation.
In recent years, the shift from print to digital has impacted how we learn. Just as the printing press became a major vehicle of information six centuries ago, and still is, this

Vocabulaire

Knowledge understanding
Dissemination spreading
Enables allows
Renewing itself getting new again
Training course
Crowdsourcing collaborative production
Digitization computerization
Heritage patrimony
Mindset way of thinking

transition is transforming formal education and increasing learning opportunities. Digital learning tools are rapidly increasing information sharing and enable students to develop effective self-directed learning skills. Students are able to identify what they need to learn, find and use online resources, and apply the information on the problem at hand.

Education

Culture and education differ around the world. The United States and the United Kingdom may share the same language but their cultural differences can make the two places feel as if they're worlds **apart**.
If you grew up in the United States, your youth was filled with over **zealous** holidays, learning to drive automatic cars as a teen on long straight roads to get to one of the numerous fast food **drive-thru** where you would order a medium coke that is equivalent to a large one in Europe, with a lot of ice in your beverage.
When you are a student in the United States, high school dances are a huge deal and everybody wants to be the **prom** king or **homecoming** queen. Applying to college is this massive, difficult process that's **thrilling** and terrifying at the same time.
Education systems are different in terms of equality of opportunities; there are differences between **curriculums**, differences in the interpretation of history according to the community.
The United Kingdom is increasing the proportion of students benefiting from international experience as part of their studies. It faces the challenge of a **brain drain** of educated British citizens, so the United Kingdom is taking step to both attract and retain **high-skilled** talents.

Companies

Companies contribute to the collaborative production of knowledge. They can work in partnership with schools and universities, such as Californian **IT** companies which collaborate with CalTech (California Institute of Technology). It is no secret that the Silicon Valley harbors the most successful self-taught tech founders. Nevertheless, firms are blamed for the ethical impact of the management of the data and algorithms e.g. **recommender** systems that are used in a variety of areas: playlist generators for video and music services like Netflix, YouTube and Spotify, product recommenders for services such as Amazon, or content recommenders for social media platforms such as Facebook and Twitter.

Vocabulaire

Apart separated
Zealous enthusiastic
Drive-thru drive-through/takeaway restaurant
Prom graduation ball
Homecoming high school event with former students
Thrilling exciting
Curriculums courses
Brain drain mass emigration of skilled people
High-skilled very qualified
IT information technology
Recommender information filtering

Actualité

The ongoing crisis related to the COVID-19 pandemic forces many firms to introduce teleworking on a large scale and universities have transitioned from face-to-face to distance learning. Stanford University, with over 20 years of experience in online learning, as well as MOOCs (Massive Open Online Courses), has improved online learning platforms and pedagogies.
What did online learning change for you?

Exercices

01 Reading

'DEEPLY CONCERNING': **FIGURES** REVEAL BREXIT THREAT AS 11,000 EU **ACADEMICS** LEAVE UK

Just **shy of** 11,000 EU academics working in the UK have quit their .... [1] in the three years since Britain voted to leave the European Union, new figures from the **Lib Dems** have revealed.

The analysis, based on freedom of .... [2] responses from 81 universities, also showed that over 4,000 EU academics left the UK universities in the last year alone – a 31% increase on the 3,000 who left before the vote. In 2018-19, 4,014 EU academics left the UK universities compared to 3,051 in 2015-16.

Oxford, Edinburgh and Cambridge all top the .... [3] which have seen the largest number of EU academics leaving since the Brexit .... [4], with respectively 1,515, 1,271 and 1,292 EU **staff** leaving each institution.

The Liberal Democrats called the figures "deeply concerning" and added they point towards a Brexit .... [5] due to uncertainty over freedom of movement and international .... [6] funding.

Lib Dem Shadow Education Secretary Layla Moran said: "It is a deeply concerning that Brexit has already driven so many .... [7] academics to abandon the UK. Our universities are being threatened by a Brexit brain drain, exacerbated by Boris Johnson's **reckless** promise to crash us out of the EU by 2020 no matter the cost."

.... [8] also face uncertainty over their immigration status and their funding following Brexit, which could make the UK less .... [9] in attracting international talent.

The higher education **body** Universities UK already found 60% of universities **surveyed** believed they had lost existing or potential staff members because of Brexit, and other research has shown the UK's share of total EU research funding has fallen by 4.5% or nearly half a billion pounds.

"This is sadly not surprising given the **Tory** party has adopted the xenophobic rhetoric of [pro-Brexit Member of the European Parliament] **Nigel Farage**, making our .... [10], friends and family from the EU feel .... [11]" Layla Moran continued.

"It's not too late to **turn the tide** and prevent [Prime Minister] Boris Johnson imposing his divisive Brexit plans on the country."

Adapted from Matthew Nixon, the neweuropean.co.uk, 2 December 2019
Source: https://www.theneweuropean.co.uk/top-stories/liberal-democrat-figures-reveal-brexit-threat-as-11-000-eu-academics-leave-uk-1-6403909

Wordbox

Figures statistics
Academics scholars researchers
Shy of just under
Lib Dems Liberal Democrats
Staff manpower
Reckless careless
Body representative organization
Surveyed questioned
Tory conservative party
Nigel Farage Leader of the Brexit party
Turn the tide change the course

Exercices

A) Complete the text with the following words.

a) vote
b) information
c) competitive
d) unwelcome
e) brain drain
f) position
g) talented
h) academics
i) research
j) colleagues
k) universities

B) Put the main ideas of the text in the right order.

a) Academics even left the highest-ranked universities.

b) Academics are concerned about their status and the research funding.

c) The Conservative Party is inflicting contentious issues following Brexit.

d) The European Union research funding for the United Kingdom is decreasing.

e) The Liberal Democrats are worried about the brain drain caused by Brexit.

f) 11,000 academics left between 2016 and 2019.

→ ○ → ○ → ○ → ○ → ○ → ○

02 Vocabulary

Match the following words with the correct definition.

1. **Knowledge** ○ — ○ a) To be autodidact.
2. **Innovation** ○ — ○ b) The gap between those who have access to computers and those who do not.
3. **University** ○ — ○ c) Teamwork.
4. **Dissemination** ○ — ○ d) Valued things or traditions passed down from previous generations.
5. **Heritage** ○ — ○ e) A high-level educational institution.
6. **Digital divide** ○ — ○ f) The action or process of innovating.
7. **Self-taught** ○ — ○ g) Education using technology.
8. **Digital learning** ○ — ○ h) Information and skills acquired through experience or education.
9. **Collaboration** ○ — ○ i) The action or fact of spreading something (especially information) widely.

Sciences and technologies, promises and challenges

Sciences et techniques, promesses et défis

Race to innovation

Not only sciences and technologies have an impact at a national level but they are also impulsing **momentum** at an international scale. Progress **encompasses** different fields such as energy consumption, accommodation and transportation. Plus, it has its share of political, economic, environmental and social challenges.

In spite of the competition, the United States keeps a remarkable economic trend especially in the sector of technology, while the United Kingdom and Canada continue to stimulate the development of technologies and manufacturing, and try not to **lose ground** in the race to innovation despite the current **gloomy** economic situation. In this race to innovation and performance, the space industry and smartphone industry have been steadily growing and have experienced super-fast advancements.

To face the leadership of the United States in those fields, countries have intended to **foster** innovation. They have provided investments to stay competitive in plans such as Innovation for a Better Canada, in order to make Canada a world-leading center for innovation or Innovation Nation in the United Kingdom. Likewise, awards like the Nobel Prize but also Youth Innovation Award in Canada are **granted**, or initiatives as Youth Innovation Centres in Jamaica, Young Innovators of Nigeria are taken to recognize and highlight innovative, **outstanding** and sometimes revolutionary ideas.

Controversy

Capitalism, the freedom of enterprise and mass consumption underlie social and economic issues and the expansion of digital giants and e-commerce.

There are significant challenges associated with Artificial Intelligence (AI), **shale** gas, robots, augmented humans, self-driving cars, drones, magnetic levitation trains.

Transhumanism, which is the development of the human condition with technologies such as exoskeleton to enhance human physiology and intellect, is a controversial topic today. Similarly, even if the use of AI can boost competitiveness and productivity, help reduce errors, make decisions more easily and carry out actions more rapidly, consumers don't trust these technologies.

Besides, even though genetic research helps to end the spread of diseases and change characteristics through **cloning**, it may be done **in defiance of** ethics.

Vocabulaire

Momentum dynamism
Encompasses includes
Lose ground regress
Gloomy pessimistic
Foster boost
Granted given
Outstanding exceptional
Shale schist rock
Cloning genetic copying
In defiance of in spite of

Workplace

It is at the office that many people spend most of their time, that's why some companies feel like it is vital that space be designed to bring out the best in all. Some companies change the office space to be more reactive or more informational, others move towards **sustainable** practices.
Companies saw the decline of **cubicles** and the emergence of **open-plan** offices with amenities that foster social interactions. The spectacular rise of **co-working** and shared workspaces has allowed larger firms to become more adaptable and collaborative, empowering a more independent and entrepreneurial workforce.
Employees are allowed to choose whatever desk they like to sit at on a daily basis. The lighting system has adjustable light levels, so that it enables the workers to change the light. People migrate to the area that they want and start customizing it more.
Companies are adopting new space strategies to benefit employees such as teleworking. They commute less and use their time more efficiently. All in all, telecommuting participates in the improvement of the family well-being and in reducing the environmental footprint.
Today, a clean energy revolution is taking place across the world, whether it is in New Zealand with the wind energy or in Australia with the solar energy. In addition, companies in Canada and in the United Kingdom are **implementing ground-breaking** innovations to limit carbon dioxide emissions.

Entertainment

The film industry is the child of an era when modern science and modern society were formed. Cinema was not only a modern technological invention of the end of the 19th century, but it also became a modern social practice.
In recent years, technologies such as the autonomous drones, 3D, computer animation and streaming have contributed to reshape the film industry. In parallel, a rather **thought-provoking** change in the video game industry is the expanding amount of gamers who are looking for easier ways to access games and creating a demand for more immersive entertainments.
According to the age group, there is also a growing interest in social media that has led to a declining interest in television: people report they usually multitask with an Internet-connected device while watching television.

Vocabulaire

- **Sustainable** environmentally friendly
- **Cubicles** small workspace
- **Open-plan** without walls
- **Co-working** sharing an office with employees of different companies
- **Implementing** carrying out
- **Ground-breaking** advanced
- **Thought-provoking** interesting

Actualité

To maintain social-distancing, Broadway theaters abruptly closed. They are heading towards a showdown that forces them to innovate in social media marketing, show production and staging. In 2021, BroadwayCon, the biggest fan convention dedicated to Broadway performances, is held online.

Exercices

01 Civilization

Watch this video and answer the following questions.

Source : *Newsweek*, "How Netflix changed TV".

https://www.youtube.com/watch?v=XL6zNexyt8o

1) How many subscribers does Netflix have?
- ❑ **a.** 100 million
- ❑ **b.** 50 million

2) Where does it operate?
- ❑ **a.** In 119 countries
- ❑ **b.** In 190 countries

3) What was the initial service provided?
- ❑ **a.** Blockbuster DVD rental service
- ❑ **b.** Mail order DVD service

4) What was the innovation in 2007?
- ❑ **a.** Internet video on demand
- ❑ **b.** Delivering its billionth DVD

5) What does "binge watching" mean?
- ❑ **a.** Watching an entire season in one go
- ❑ **b.** Airing episodes weekly

6) What are the other factors that helped Netflix's growth?
- ❑ **a.** Improvement in streaming technology and rise of handled devices
- ❑ **b.** None of the content belonged to Netflix

7) What was the solution to the problem of copyright?
- ❑ **a.** Attract top Hollywood talents to work on web TV series
- ❑ **b.** Produce their own online-only television series

8) How many original programs did it run in 2016?
- ❑ **a.** 126
- ❑ **b.** 147

9) What are its future prospects to face competition?
- ❑ **a.** Double original programming
- ❑ **b.** Triple original programming

10) What could it venture into in the future?
- ❑ **a.** Unscripted content
- ❑ **b.** Live TV

02 Vocabulary

Fill in the crossword.

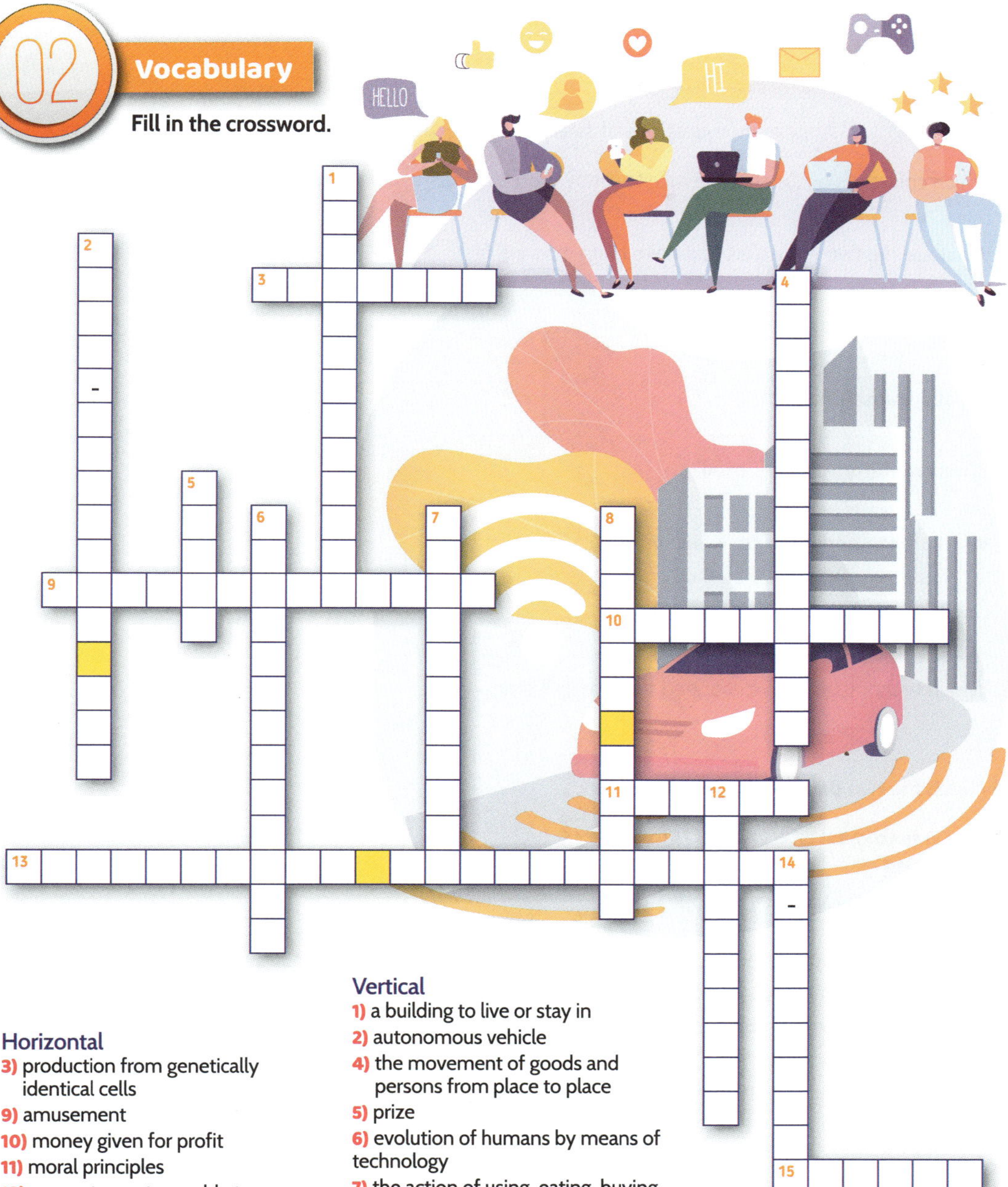

Horizontal

3) production from genetically identical cells
9) amusement
10) money given for profit
11) moral principles
13) computer systems able to perform tasks normally requiring human intelligence
15) power derived from the use of resources

Vertical

1) a building to live or stay in
2) autonomous vehicle
4) the movement of goods and persons from place to place
5) prize
6) evolution of humans by means of technology
7) the action of using, eating, buying
8) applications and websites to participate in social networking
12) invention
14) online trade

Exercices

03 Understanding

A) Answer the questions of sciences and technologies.

1) Which country is a leader in the race to innovation?

....

2) What are the two industries that have been growing fast?

....

3) Which countries are intending to foster innovation?

....

4) What is transhumanism?

....

5) What are the advantages of AI?

....

6) What are the benefit of co-working?

....

7) What are the upsides of teleworking?

....

8) Which technologies have changed the film industry?

....

B) Match the two parts of the sentences.

Some tips to master working from home.

1) Organize your workspace without distractions...
2) Use ergonomic work furniture...
3) Secure your Internet connection...
4) Give yourself a fixed schedule...
5) Set daily goals and tasks...
6) Optimize communication with the team...

a) ◯ ... to collaborate effectively.
b) ◯ ... to maintain a comfortable and neutral body posture.
c) ◯ ... to structure your days including your breaks.
d) ◯ ... to access corporate data safely.
e) ◯ ... to be able to track your work progress.
f) ◯ ... to be able to concentrate.

Synthesis: Production and circulation of knowledge

Production and circulation of knowledge

Knowledge society

- Knowledge producers i.e. schools, universities, researchers
- They disseminate knowledge to develop sciences

The digital world

- New power source of education and knowledge through constant connectivity *via* various media
- Cultural changes: collaboration, creation, heritage, language, mindset, social relations
- Digital learning has emerged
- The digital divide is a threat

Education

- Differences in culture and education between countries
- Example of a United States teenager and student
- Different education systems: inequality of opportunities and curriculums, different interpretations of history
- The increasing mobility of United Kingdom students and the brain drain

Companies

- Companies contribute to the collaborative production of knowledge
- Successful self-taught tech founders in the Silicon Valley
- Firms are blamed for the ethical impact management of the data and algorithms

Synthesis: Sciences and technologies, promises and challenges

Sciences and technologies, promises and challenges

Race to innovation

- Progress includes various fields and challenges
- The race to innovation between countries such as the United States, the United Kingdom and Canada
- The space industry and smartphone industry is flourishing
- Countries invest in plans to facilitate innovation

Controversy

- Social and economic issues due to capitalism
- Innovations like transhumanism and AI are controversial
- The ethical challenges of genetic research

Clean energy

- Human society's dependence on energy and use of resources
- Environmental changes
- Clean energy revolution with initiatives in New Zealand, Australia, Canada and the United Kingdom

Entertainment

- The reshaping of the film industry
- The changes of the video game industry
- Social media vs television

☑ **Première**
☐ Terminale

Representations

Représentations

- **Make one's voice heard: representation and participation**
  Faire entendre sa voix : représentation et participation
- **Inform and get informed**
  Informer et s'informer
- **Represent the world and represent oneself**
  Représenter le monde et se représenter

Make one's voice heard: representation and participation

Faire entendre sa voix : représentation et participation

Monarchy

The United Kingdom is a constitutional monarchy in which the **reigning** monarch (King or Queen) is the head of state, while the Prime Minister of the United Kingdom is the head of government. The Crown has lost some of its powers but is a personification of the state itself. The political decisions are taken by the government and the **bicameral** Parliament consisting of the House of Commons and the House of Lords. The latter is said to be undemocratic owing to the fact that it is made up of, for example, **bishops** and hereditary **peers**, that they are wholly **unaccountable** to the United Kingdom's citizens. In other words, the recent modernization of the monarchy includes bringing it closer to the people.

Today, the Commonwealth is an association of 54 independent countries, vestige of Great Britain's former colonial empire. The Crown is actually the monarch of 16 different countries that are part of the Commonwealth realm: Australia, Belize, Canada, New Zealand, and other smaller Commonwealth **realms**. These include several island nations in the Caribbean such as Jamaica and the Bahamas, or Papua New Guinea and Tuvalu in the Pacific Ocean.

Democracies

Just because most English-speaking countries are democracies doesn't mean they have the same political representation, legislative process, as well as government, voting and referendum systems; or counter-powers like **trade unions**, lobbies and associations. In contrast to the United Kingdom, countries like the United States, India and South Africa have presidents as the head of state and head of government.

South Africa has the most progressive constitution since 1996, when anti-**apartheid** revolutionary leader Nelson Mandela **promulgated**. The United States is a federal government which shares **sovereignty** with the 50 state governments. It is a country, though it is, by and large, not considered as a nation.

Hong Kong is strikingly a former British colony where democratic rights have been major issues since the **handover** to China in 1997: a series of protests, called the Umbrella Revolution, in 2014 regarding reforms to the Hong Kong electoral system and the ongoing protests were triggered by an amendment bill, exposing people to the legal system of mainland China, thereby **undermining** Hong Kong's autonomy and infringing civil liberties.

The Republic of Ireland, also known as Éire was created, following a civil war, as the Irish Free State in 1922 and had the status of dominion until 1937 when a new constitution was adopted, with an elected president as head of state.

Vocabulaire

- **Reigning** ruling
- **Bicameral** with two chambers
- **Bishops** clergymen
- **Peers** aristocrats
- **Unaccountable** answerable
- **Realms** kingdoms
- **Trade unions** worker's syndicate
- **Apartheid** segregation system (in South Africa)
- **Promulgated** introduced
- **Sovereignty** autonomy
- **Handover** transfer of sovereignty
- **Undermining** weakening

Devolution

There are also devolved Scottish and Welsh Parliaments and a devolved Assembly in Northern Ireland, with varying degrees of legislative authority. Originally, a referendum was held in Northern Ireland in 1998 and a **landslide** majority of voters were in favor of devolution, that is to say the transfer of power from England to the other members of the union (Scotland, Wales, and Northern Ireland). It progressively has somehow removed the unitary veil from Britain's union structure to make explicit the quasi-federal relationship between Westminster and the new devolved governments. These are new and powerful symbols of **nationhood**, which raise the question of sovereignty and **sharpen** people's sense of dual identity, with people seeing themselves as Scottish, Welsh, Irish or English as well as British.

Elections

It is standard to describe the United States presidential contest as **divisive**. The president is elected indirectly by the people of each state, through an Electoral College. The Electoral College has unmistakably its issues, from the increasing frequency of presidents winning the election while losing the popular vote to the millions of voters in some states who know that their votes make no practical difference in the election because their state is underrepresented. Basically, the winner-take-all system of vote has unacceptable anti-democratic effects because it translates millions of votes within a state into zero, which means it does not **comply with** "one person, one vote".
On top of that, the federal government has also been involved in attempts to increase voter **turnout** unfairly. Not to mention, the private financing of campaign has also long been controversial, because sources make up more than substantial amounts of money.

Vocabulaire

- **Landslide** great
- **Nationhood** independency
- **Sharpen** make clearer
- **Divisive** conflictful
- **Comply with** be conform with
- **Turnout** participation

Actualité

After the 2020 United States presidential election in which Biden prevailed, incumbent Trump and his supporter pursued an aggressive, unprecedented effort to overturn the election. It lead to a violent attack against the Capitol on January 6, 2021 by the supporters. In response to the assault, various social media companies banned President Trump from using their platforms.

Exercices

01 Civilization

Hong Kong, 2016.

1) What is the man doing?
- ❑ **a.** He is an activist calling on pedestrians to join a protest
- ❑ **b.** He is a famous celebrity surrounded by paparazzi

2) Who is Nelson Mandela?
- ❑ **a.** A revolutionary Hongkongese leader
- ❑ **b.** A revolutionary South African leader

3) What does the quote refer to?
- ❑ **a.** The Anti-Apartheid Revolution
- ❑ **b.** The Umbrella Revolution

4) To which country does Hong Kong is a part of today?
- ❑ **a.** China
- ❑ **b.** The United Kingdom

5) When was the handover of Hong Kong to China?
- ❑ **a.** 1997
- ❑ **b.** 2014

6) What is the Umbrella Revolution?
- ❑ **a.** A takeover of the government
- ❑ **b.** A series of protests

7) Why do Hongkongers protest in 2014?
- ❑ **a.** To protest regarding reforms to the electoral system
- ❑ **b.** To protest regarding an amendment bill hindering Hong Kong's autonomy

8) Which other country withdrew for British rule in 1922?
- ❑ **a.** The Republic of Ireland
- ❑ **b.** Northern Ireland

9) Who is the head of state of Éire?
- ❑ **a.** The British monarch
- ❑ **b.** A president

10) How many countries are in the Commonwealth?
- ❑ **a.** 16
- ❑ **b.** 54

02 Vocabulary

A) Complete the text with the following words.

a) vice-president • b) referendums • c) parties • d) voters • e) presidential • f) democrats • g) legislation • h) campaign • i) candidate • j) landslide

I) The two political .... [1] in the United States are the Republicans and the .... [2]

II) The .... [3] for the next election usually comes with several .... [4] promises.

III) Unlike in other United States elections, the president and .... [5] are not elected directly by the .... [6] .

IV) .... [7], by contrast, allow citizens to vote directly on .... [8] .

V) Most .... [9] elections are very close, there is never a .... [10] majority.

B) Translate these sentences into English.

a) Il est bien connu que la monarchie est la plus ancienne institution en Grande-Bretagne et est le symbole de l'identité britannique.

....

....

....

....

b) La monarchie fait écho à l'idée de tradition et incarne les espoirs et les croyances des britanniques.

....

....

....

c) Des débats publics ont divisé la nation en deux groupes : les monarchistes et les républicains.

....

....

d) Les situations délicates souffertes par la famille Windsor sont considérées comme une crise résultante du conflit entre tradition et modernité.

....

....

....

e) Le monarque britannique est déterminé à protéger sa neutralité politique pour représenter le pays entier.

....

....

....

C) Match the word with its definition.

1 Referendum	○	○	The site of the British Houses of Parliament. a
2 Devolution	○	○	A text of fundamental principles according to which a state is governed. b
3 Westminster	○	○	A general vote by the electorate on a single political question. c
4 Éire	○	○	The territory of a sovereign government. d
5 Dominion	○	○	An association of countries that were previously part of the British Empire. e
6 Constitution	○	○	The Irish name for Ireland. f
7 Commonwealth	○	○	The transfer of power from the central government to regional administration. g

Inform and get informed

Informer et s'informer

The role of the media

Our world is more and more a single information society where media is a part of everyone's life and plays a major role in society as a source of information. The purpose of a media is to give information about current public debates, news and **gossips**, thanks to which people can gain knowledge and have a **depiction** of the political, economic and social challenges, and of the world in general.
Society is influenced by media in numerous ways. It is the mass media that helps individuals to get information about a multitude of things, form opinions and make a judgment regarding various issues: it keeps people updated and informed about what is happening around them.

Types of media

Print media is one of the oldest and basic forms of communication. It includes newspapers, books, weeklies, magazines, monthlies, posters and other forms of printed material. In the United Kingdom, **polarization** has been between the quality press and the popular press. The quality press referred to as **broadsheets** includes news **outlets** like *The Time*, *The Guardian* and *The Independent*, etc. The popular press, known as the **tabloids** like *The Sun* or *the Daily Mirror*, attracts the reader's attention with sensational headlines often about celebrity gossip. It is criticized for **encroaching** in the private life of people.
The decline of the press didn't start with the emergence of radio but when television **superseded** it. Television, as the world's most powerful medium of communication, is a key part of that society. Television can be a tremendous force for good. It can educate great numbers of people about the world around them.
The spread of mobile media devices, such as smartphones and tablet computers, has been markedly rapid around the world in the recent years. Mobile media became a crucial part of everyone's life. The user can use his latest gadget anywhere by carrying it in his pocket. He can enjoy a wide variety of programs and, most importantly, share content. Mobile media has challenged the traditional media use and modified human interaction.

Vocabulaire

Gossips rumors
Depiction image
Polarization divergence
Broadsheets large-format newspapers
Outlets media
Tabloids small-formats newspapers
Encroaching invading
Superseded took the place of

Democracy

It is the **backbone** of a democracy. It is based on the freedom of the press, that is the principle that expression through various media should be exercised freely, without the interference from a controlling state. The media exposes flaws in the democratic system, which ultimately helps government in making the system more **accountable**, responsive and citizen-friendly. Whistleblowing draws public attention to perceive the **wrongdoing** of an organization or government. It is the fourth **pillars** of democracy, and as such it ensures that all people living in rural areas of the country are aware of what's happening in the rest of their country. Media can be considered as a **watchdog** of political democracy.
The media affects people's perspective by filtering the information received and presenting it in a way which they believe best represents the story. Whoever controls the media controls the mind. Too much intervention of media in everything is a matter of concern.

Social media in politics

The use of online social media platforms has rapidly grown in importance as a forum for political activism in its different forms. Social media platforms provide new ways to stimulate citizen engagement in political life. Communication with **spin doctors** *via* social media brings politicians and parties closer to their potential voters.
It also helps customize messages, adapt political narratives or publish fake news. During a political campaign, fake news can give a misleading information in order to tarnish the reputation of a candidate. It is very decisive in winning the vote.
However, direct access to voters also has its **downsides**. Public-relations professionals often manage a candidate's image, **landing** public figures in embarrassing situations.
Moreover, it weighs the public opinion instantaneously. This way, politicians can then adjust, or **scrub** anything unflattering. Social media tools have allowed to easily gather and even to petition the government, **leveraging** powerful lobbyists.

Vocabulaire

Backbone basis
Accountable responsible

Wrongdoing misconduct
Pillars basis
Watchdog defender
Spin doctors press agents

Downsides drawbacks
Landing putting
Scrub erase
Leveraging influencing

Actualité

One of the reasons Hillary Clinton lost the 2016 election is because, during the campaign, the storytelling and fake news from the media revolved around the Hillary Clinton email controversy. When she worked as United States Secretary of State, she violated the law by using a private email account for official communications rather than using official secure federal email account. The controversy received more media coverage than any other topic during the presidential campaign.

Exercices

01 Reading

TRUMP'S 'FAKE NEWS' **CRUSADE** IS RIGHT OUT OF DICTATOR PLAYBOOK

The president of the United States has now declared that CNN, NBC, CBS and ABC along with the "failing" *New York Times* and *The Washington Post* are not news organizations staffed by professional journalists but **mere** fabricators of **baseless** information. "They are all Fake News!" Donald Trump wrote in yet another wildly unpresidential Twitter **salvo**.

Let's pause to appreciate what this means: the president of the United States is issuing a **blanket** declaration that six of the most prominent and respected news ...... [1] in the country are not to be ...... [2].

The story citing one ...... [3] source, claimed the Senate intelligence committee was looking into a meeting between the head of a Russian investment fund and Trump ally Anthony Scaramucci shortly before Trump took office.

Saying the ...... [4] did not meet the network's ...... [5] standards, CNN pulled it from the website the night after it was published and apologized to Scaramucci. The network then accepted the ...... [6] of the three ...... [7] involved in the piece.

That doesn't sound like something a ...... [8] network would do. It sounds like a news organization taking **swift** responsibility for their errors and journalists taking responsibility for their actions.

Scaramucci seemed to think so as well, responding *via* Twitter: "CNN did the right thing. Classy move. Apology accepted. Everyone makes mistakes. Moving on". But apparently the president didn't get the memo about moving on.

Then White House deputy press secretary Sarah Huckabee Sanders continued the "fake news media" **blasting** during Tuesday's press briefing after she was asked why the CNN resignations weren't enough to calm the president's **ire**. "I think it's the constant barrage of fake news that is directed at this president, probably, that has **garnered** a lot of his frustration," she said.

There are many problems inherent in those two comments. For starters, you'll note that something is only "fake news" when it's critical of President Trump. Was the *New York Times* story that broke the news that Hillary Clinton used a private email account while serving as secretary of state fake news? No. Were those made-up sources? Or are those solid ...... [9] because it's a story Trump can use to shape his own ...... [10]?

Journalists, like anyone else, are capable of lying or making stuff up. But when that happens, we end up out of a job. Consider these words from Hannah Arendt, an American political theorist who wrote extensively about totalitarianism: "A people that no longer can believe anything cannot make up its mind. It is **deprived** not only of its capacity to act but also of its capacity to think and to judge. And with such a people you can then do what you please."

Adapted from Rex W. Huppke, chicagotribune.com, 2019.
Source: https://digitaledition.chicagotribune.com/tribune/article_popover.aspx?guid=fa678762-dd25-41fe-828e-7e237df6a226

Exercices

A) Complete the text with the following words.

- a) journalists
- b) trusted
- c) outlets
- d) resignations
- e) fake news
- f) anonymous
- g) sources
- h) narrative
- i) editorial
- j) story

Wordbox

- **Crusade** offensive
- **Mere** just
- **Baseless** without sources
- **Salvo** verbal attack
- **Blanket** general
- **Swift** fast
- **Blasting** fuss
- **Ire** anger
- **Garnered** gathered
- **Deprived** lacking

B) Put the main ideas of the text in the right order.

- a) The president uses fake news for its political narrative.
- b) Unlike Scaramucci, the president kept on making a fuss about the story.
- c) CNN denounced a connection between a Russian investor and the president's ally Scaramucci.
- d) The accusations of fake news of the president undermining news outlets professionalism.
- e) CNN apologized for the journalists' lack of fact-checking.

○ → ○ → ○ → ○ → ○

C) What is the author's point of view? Answer these questions.

1) The president of the United States is right to accuse six news outlets in the country because they surely shouldn't be trusted. ○ Right ○ Wrong

2) CNN took immediate responsibility which implies it acted professionally. ○ Right ○ Wrong

3) Successful journalists are those who publish fake news with no sources. ○ Right ○ Wrong

4) The press can manipulate people. ○ Right ○ Wrong

5) News that criticize Trump are necessarily fake. ○ Right ○ Wrong

Represent the world and represent oneself

Représenter le monde et se représenter

Soft power

The act of representing **conveys** a multitude of ideas through various channels. The **artworks span** cinema, painting, music, literature, the performing arts (theater, dance, opera, street theater), or architecture.

Art helps shape the past, the present and the future. It is a soft power that affects the ways in which people both think and act.

People from the same nation share the same cultural identity through art. National myths, such as the stereotypical American Dream, often serve as important national symbols and instill national values. The example of the United States shows that the stereotypes conveyed by art can evolve into anti-Americanism.

It can even take the form of protests, addressing political and social issues with direct action. There is no doubt that art movements can change society: socially engaged art is a medium of denunciation through caricature. Many movements in art history have tried to depict or even change society in one way or another: whether it is literature with well-known authors like Paul Auster, Sherman Alexie, Jonathan Coe, Arundhati Roy, J. M. Coetzee, Nadine Gordimer, Siri Hustvedt, etc. or architecture like the impressive city landscapes of London or New York or the distinctive opera of Sydney in the no less unique country-continent, Australia.

Moreover, commercial or institutional advertising also contributes to shape our culture since the media have an impact on the public opinion. Some **iconic** ad campaigns have changed our way of life: the reason why we drink orange juice for breakfast or the idea we have of Santa Claus can be traced back to popular ads.

Cinema

Heritage films are **period** films which depict the United Kingdom, mostly, in a nostalgic fashion with splendid scenes of the English landscape. It is the official promotion of a prosperous, powerful and socially **cohesive** nation and an upper-class-**biased** notion of the British heritage.

Award-winning English filmmaker Ken Loach genuinely portrays working-class people. His socially critical directing style and socialist ideals are obvious in his film treatment of social issues such as poverty, homelessness and labor rights.

Going still further, films can become effective propaganda tools and are produced to convince the viewer of a specific political point or mobilize people for a common cause. They can influence the opinions of the viewer by providing subjective content that may be deliberately **misleading**.

Cinema today has become a global cultural form. At the same time as Hollywood is a reflection of the American society, American cultural hegemony operates through films, imposing standards to the world. Similarly, other industries are emerging in India, nicknamed Bollywood, and in Nigeria, called Nollywood.

Vocabulaire

Conveys gives
Artworks pieces of art
Span cover
Iconic emblematic
Period history
Cohesive coherent
Biased partial
Misleading confusing

Music

Music has become an archetypal conduit for expression.

In the 1960s, Bob Dylan was a pioneer and a major figure in American popular culture. Some songs became **anthems** for the civil rights and anti-war movements with lyrics incorporating a range of political ideals and appealing to the **burgeoning** counterculture.

In 2018, the UNESCO (United Nations Educational, Scientific and Cultural Organization) inscribed reggae into its list of heritage. Reggae originated in Jamaica in the late 1960s and has an enduring popularity. Reggae icon, Bob Marley went from being a pioneering Jamaican reggae singer to an international superstar of an unprecedented popularity, promoting Rastafari beliefs and Pan-Africanism.

Emerging in the United States in the 1970s, rap music and culture, commonly associated with hip hop and spoken-word poetry, have been an open window on the ghettos.

Painting

Artists use painting to depict the world. Faith Ringgold is an American painter, writer and performance artist, best known for her bold narrative **quilts** in the 1970s. Many of her provocative artworks focus on racial interactions from a female point of view and call basic racial issues in America into question. In another way, Hew Locke, a Scottish artist who uses a wide range of media and makes extensive use of found objects, produced a series called *House of Windsor* which consists of portraits of members of the British royal family.

The graffiti movement appeared as one of the logical continuations of the Pop artistic tendencies, but this urban style has very much grown since. Street art was brought to light by Keith Haring and Basquiat, who were widely influenced by Pop Art. Urban art is deeply rooted in the idea that many street artists claim we do not live in a museum so art should be in public places. That's why, it is actually created in public locations. Some artists use this vandalism as a way to raise awareness about social and political issues.

Provocative and **controversial** art put your commitment to free speech to the test and is a **corollary** to a free society based on the principle that every individual has the right to decide what art or **entertainment** he or she wants to receive or create.

Vocabulaire

Anthems official song of a country
Burgeoning developing
Quilts patchworks
Controversial disputed
Corollary consequence
Entertainment amusement

Actualité

Banksy is an English-based graffiti artist and activist who uses anonymity and art as political weapons. He keeps his identity closely guarded but he is regularly making headlines. His subversive and illicit street art combines satire with graffiti and deals with various political and social themes, as a form of guerilla that allows an individual to snatch away power and territory.

Exercices

01 Civilization

Watch this video and answer the questions.

Source : BBC, "Giant koala sand art captures Australian bushfires emotions"

https://www.bbc.com/news/av/world-australia-51217664/giant-koala-sand-art-captures-australian-bushfires-emotions

1) The main topic of this video is:
- ❑ **a.** bushfires
- ❑ **b.** extinction of species

2) What did he look at?
- ❑ **a.** Smog
- ❑ **b.** Smoke

3) What can he smell?
- ❑ **a.** Fires that are up to hundreds kilometers away
- ❑ **b.** Fires that are up two hundred kilometers away

4) He feels a sense of ...?
- ❑ **a.** helplessness
- ❑ **b.** helpfulness

5) Why did he choose to depict a koala according to you?
- ❑ **a.** Koalas epitomize Australia
- ❑ **b.** Bushfires have taken the lives of thousands of koalas

6) How does he capture the image?
- ❑ **a.** With a drone
- ❑ **b.** With a rake

7) He uses sand art in order to...
- ❑ **a.** verbalize his emotions
- ❑ **b.** visualize his emotions

8) What is the common point between Banksy and Edward?
- ❑ **a.** Animosity
- ❑ **b.** Anonymity

9) Why did he draw a firefighter?
- ❑ **a.** To keep the community safe
- ❑ **b.** To pay tribute

10) What is the cause of the bushfires?
- ❑ **a.** Drought
- ❑ **b.** Flood

02 Vocabulary

Fill in the crossword.

Horizontal

4) a drawing representing a person, where some characteristics are exaggerated
7) biased information given to promote certain ideas
8) a theater where movies are shown
10) nonrural
11) a person who campaigns for political or social changes
13) amusement
14) the art or practice of designing buildings

Vertical

1) drawing on public walls
2) written works, considered to be an art form, such as prose, drama and poetry
3) a series of movements rhythmically to music
5) a way of life opposed to the prevailing social norms
6) a painting, drawing or photograph of a person, especially of the face
9) voice and/or instrumental sound
11) a piece of art
12) explorer or innovator

Synthesis: Make one's voice heard: representation and participation

Make one's voice heard: representation and participation

Monarchy

- The United Kingdom is a constitutional monarchy with a monarch who has fewer powers than the Prime Minister
- The House of Lords is considered undemocratic since its members are not representative of the population
- The Crown rules over 16 different countries

Democracies

- English-speaking democracies differ from one another
- The United States, India and South Africa have presidents
- South Africa has the most progressive constitution
- The United States is a federal government but is sometimes not considered as a nation
- Hong Kong faces major issues since the handover
- Ireland became independent from the the United Kingdom in 1922

Elections

- The United States presidential contest as divisive
- Some states are underrepresented. The winner-take-all system doesn't correspond to the popular vote
- Issues with the actions increasing voter's participation and with the financing and the campaigns

Devolution

- Devolved institutions in Scotland, Wales and Northern Ireland following a referendum
- New structure of the United Kingdom with more autonomy and regional identity

Synthesis: Inform and get informed

Inform and get informed

The role of the media

- Source of information
- Depiction of the political, economic and social challenges as the world in general

Types of media

- The press, the oldest form of communication
- In the United Kingdom: the broadsheets and the tabloids
- Radio and the most powerful media: television
- The rise of mobile media

Democracy

- Whistleblowing to alert the public
- The fourth pillar of democracy: a watchdog
- The media choose the way they present a story

Social media in politics

- Political activism to stimulate voters
- The use of customized message, political narratives and fake news
- Positive or negative image of the politician
- A tool to influence the government or lobbyists

Synthesis: Represent the world and represent oneself

Represent the world and represent oneself

Soft power

- The act of representing conveys ideas *via* cinema, painting, music, literature, the performing arts or architecture
- It depicts the world and is a power that influences people
- Advertising shapes our culture

Cinema

- Heritage films depict a prosperous United Kingdom, in a nostalgic way
- Ken Loach's films portray working-class people
- Films can become effective propaganda tools

Music

- A form of expression
- Bob Dylan: a pioneer of counterculture
- The popularity of reggae and the promotion of Pan-Africanism
- Rap and hip hop music from the ghettos

Painting

- Faith Ringgold: provocative artwork focused on racial issues
- Hew Locke: portraits of members of the British royal family
- Street art is an anti-museum urban art based on vandalism, and supports free speech
- Banksy: street art as a tool for activism

☐ Première

☑ Terminale

Be a society

Faire société

- **Unity and plurality**
  Unité et pluralité
- **Public liberties and individual liberties**
  Libertés publiques et libertés individuelles
- **Equalities and inequalities**
  Égalités et inégalités

Unity and plurality

Unité et pluralité

Unity in plurality

English is the official language in around 50 countries and the plurality of these English-speaking countries has attracted people looking for new horizons, often viewed as an El Dorados, or has generated different kinds of **diaspora**, based on its causes such as colonialism, trade, or labor migrations.
Cultural plurality and mobility can **undermine** unity but can also be a source of renewal, with the cultural **intermingling**. It corresponds for example to the adaptation made by minorities such as immigrants, refugees, and indigenous people in response to their contact with the dominant majority.
Unfortunately, culture **clashes** occur when people's **expectations** coming from their cultural backgrounds are not met. It is a virtual barrier caused by cultural differences that **hinders** interactions and harmonious exchanges between people of different cultures.
Plurality is nothing but unity in the plural number. In that case, multiculturalism allows people from one culture to share information regarding their own culture, which helps other cultures to understand its **singularity**: certain traditions, practices, stereotypes, folklore and cultural heritage. It contributes to decrease racial discrimination.

From the melting-pot to the salad bowl

American identity is centered upon the melting-pot i.e. the assimilation of immigrants. The newly arrived immigrants on Ellis Island would **gaze** across the bay at the Statue of Liberty on which the pedestal bears a poem of Emma Lazarus referring to them as "*huddled masses yearning to breathe free*". The poem was quoted by John F. Kennedy in 1958 as well as in a 2010 political speech made by President Obama **advocating** immigration policy reform. In the 1960s, minorities popularized ethic pride and fought for their rights: Hispanics decided they would keep speaking Spanish. The phenomenon, called the salad bowl, means that a multicultural society can integrate different cultures while maintaining their separate identities. Today, the white share of the population is declining as Hispanic, Asian and black populations grow. The shift to a more diverse nation is happening more quickly in states such as California, Florida, and Texas.

Vocabulaire

Diaspora migration
Undermine affect
Intermingling mix
Clashes conflicts
Expectations prospects
Hinders is an obstacle to
Singularity distinctiveness
Gaze contemplate
Advocating claiming

Language

Language is one of the key to understand a culture. Speaking the national language defines national identity, as well as regional dialects contribute to distinguish the local populations. Language is one of the most important identifiers of a nation or culture. It determines the way people think, communicate and express their opinions.

Language is conditioned by the distinction between public space and private space. Language **register** in English is the **scale** of formality used to address people in different situations, it can be formal, neutral, informal and vulgar as **slang** for example. High formal is the level of language used on formal occasions to address the Queen or the Prime Minister.
As a matter of fact, accent can **trigger** social categorization. The Queen's English is considered to be the language of elites and royalty. While some people find regional accents to sound less honest or even less educated, others think they sound friendlier and that **posh** accents are more arrogant.
Interestingly enough, even if Cockney English was traditionally spoken by **working-class** Londoners, this dialect is not necessarily correlated to whom the person is and can change over time depending on social circles and daily relationships.

Separatism

The impact of language is also on the support for separatist movements such as the Language Act which put the Welsh language on an equal **footing** with the English language in Wales.
Although Canada is a predominantly English-speaking country, there are francophone communities throughout its provinces. In fact, French is the native language of about 20 percent of the total population. Most native French-speakers live in Quebec, where it is the majority official language.
In South Africa for instance, Afrikaans evolved as the **mother tongue** of Afrikaners, the descendants of the Dutch settlers. Apartheid authorities found out they could control the black population by giving them only access to Afrikaner resources instead of giving them access to a global language i.e. English. In the 1970s, during Soweto uprising, black schoolchildren protested against being taught in Afrikaans and 176 children died for the right to be taught in English. It became a turning point in the fall of Apartheid in 1994.

Religion

Religious conflict has a long history. Some English-speaking countries have various religious communities and that get involved in conflicts. Since 1947, Kashmir has been claimed by both India and Pakistan. They have been locked in conflict over Kashmir, a majority-muslim region in the northernmost part of India.
Ireland has two main religious groups. The majority of Irish are catholic, and a smaller number are protestant, mostly in the northern province of Ulster. After the Irish War of Independence (1919-1921), the British government was prepared to grant home rule to Ireland and partition between Ulster and the south took place. Actually, the territory that became Ulster had a protestant and unionist majority who wanted to maintain ties to Britain whereas the rest of Ireland had a Catholic and Irish nationalist majority who wanted independence.

Vocabulaire

- **Register** level of formality
- **Scale** range
- **Slang** informal speech
- **Trigger** start
- **Posh** elegant
- **Working-class** of laboring classes
- **Footing** position
- **Mother tongue** native language

Actualité

In 2014, a referendum took place in Scotland about Scottish independence from the United Kingdom. Prominent issues raised during the referendum including what currency an independent Scotland would use and EU membership. A majority voted against, thus Scotland remained part of the United Kingdom. Today, Brexit pushes more Scots toward support for independence.

Exercices

01 Civilization

1) To which country this image refers to?
- ❑ **a.** The United Kingdom
- ❑ **b.** The United States of America

2) Who first used this expression "a nation of immigrants"?
- ❑ **a.** John F. Kennedy
- ❑ **b.** Barack Obama

3) What does the expression "a nation of immigrants" mean?
- ❑ **a.** The nation was built with several waves of immigration
- ❑ **b.** The nation is attractive for immigrants

4) Where would immigrants arrive?
- ❑ **a.** Liberty island
- ❑ **b.** Ellis island

5) Who first used this expression "huddled masses" that is written on the Statue of Liberty?
- ❑ **a.** John F. Kennedy
- ❑ **b.** Emma Lazarus

6) What is the melting-pot?
- ❑ **a.** A society which assimilates immigrants
- ❑ **b.** A society which maintains identities

7) Which President used the expression "a nation of immigrant" to advocate immigration policy reform in 2010?
- ❑ **a.** Barack Obama
- ❑ **b.** Donald Trump

8) What is the Salad Bowl?
- ❑ **a.** A multicultural society
- ❑ **b.** A society that disintegrates

9) What is the future of white population in the USA, compared to Hispanic, Asian and black populations?
- ❑ **a.** It is rising
- ❑ **b.** It is declining

10) Which States are more diverse?
- ❑ **a.** New York State, New Jersey, Pennsylvania
- ❑ **b.** California, Florida, Texas

02 Vocabulary

A) Complete the text with the following words.

a) heritage • b) population • c) multiracial • d) ethnic • e) minority • f) melting-pot • g) income • h) education • i) culture • j) white

The 20th century has witnessed the transformation of the United States from a predominately .... [1] population rooted in Western .... [2] to a society with a variety of racial and .... [3] minorities.
As it happens, the concept of .... [4] is likely to have a very different meaning by the end of the 21st century. Hispanics, African and Asian Americans, American Indians together will make up close to half of the .... [5] It is to create a new .... [6] heritage in the United States, as a natural continuation of the .... [7] tradition, even though some view the rapid increase in ethnic minorities as a loss of America's European .... [8] Minorities have also become more diverse socioeconomically with relatively higher .... [9], access to .... [10] and representation in politics.

Source : Population Reference Bureau.

B) Translate these sentences into English.

a) La pluralité représente un éventail de différences humaines telles que l'ethnicité, la religion, le genre, l'orientation sexuelle, l'âge, le statut socio-économique ou le handicap.

....

....

....

b) La diversité présente aussi une variété de personnalités, styles de vie, opinions, compositions familiales et niveaux d'éducation.

....

....

....

c) L'unité fait référence à un sentiment d'appartenance et implique de cultiver un environnement inclusif.

....

....

d) Les sociétés deviennent de plus en plus multiculturelles et cosmopolites.

....

....

e) Une société inclusive a pour but de promouvoir l'intégration sociale, économique et politique de tous.

....

....

Public liberties and individual liberties

Libertés publiques et libertés individuelles

The land of freedom

Americans fought the War of Independence (1775-1783) in the name of freedom. As the **Pilgrim Fathers** had meant to set a model society, the **Founding Fathers** who wrote the Constitution were aware that their new nation would serve as a model of freedom. Liberty meant being free from tyranny and free from property.
All immigrants wanted to start a new life and live the American Dream. They hoped their children would climb up the social ladder. The expression "**rag** to riches" refers to any situation in which a person rises from poverty to wealth or celebrity, sometimes instantly. The poor immigrant who makes a fortune thanks to determination and hard work became the archetype of the **self-made** man. Some entrepreneurs like Levi Strauss (1829-1902), Andrew Carnegie (1835-1919) and John Davison Rockefeller (1839-1937) are emblematic of that American pioneering spirit.

Freedom of speech

Americans enjoy more freedom of expression than most democracies. All religious, philosophical, or political opinions can benefit from absolute freedom of expression according to the First Amendment of the Constitution which guarantees the freedom of speech. The Cold War (1947-1991) was an episode when the administration strangled free speech. Today, restrictions on First Amendment freedom mainly come from groups, such as the **pro-life** activists, the **political-correctness** fundamentalists or the **white supremacists**, who, in the puritan tradition, intend to impose their views.

Individual liberties

Everyone has the right to individual liberty. In the United Kingdom, during the 1960s, fertility control became more widespread with the growth of the women's movements. Unfortunately, illegal abortion was still ruining the health of many women. Women joined pro-choice associations. They campaigned effectively for the elimination of legal obstacles to abortion and the peak of their work was the Abortion Act 1967. The Act made abortion legal on a wide number of grounds in all of Great Britain (but not Northern Ireland).

Vocabulaire

- **Pilgrim Fathers** the first settlers
- **Founding Fathers** the originators of the Constitution
- **Rag** old torn clothing
- **Self-made** independently successful
- **Pro-life** opposed to abortion
- **Political-correctness** language to avoid offense
- **White supremacists** those who believe that people with pale skin are superior to others

In the Republic of Ireland, the campaign #HomeToVote urged Irish people abroad to return home to vote for same-sex marriage in 2015 and to repeal the country's abortion ban in 2018. Voters coalesced online. Thousands of citizens living outside the country were travelling back to Ireland to vote in the referendum. Both referendums passed with a landslide victory.

Separatism

Worldwide, the integrity of some people has not been respected and the emergence of federations such as South Africa, Australia, Canada, the United States, India, Malaysia, Nigeria, Pakistan, etc. or unions like the United Kingdom, have not always been accepted.
As a consequence, separatist movements have risen for instance in Quebec in Canada or in Wales, Northern Ireland, and Scotland in the United Kingdom.
It is exemplified by the 1999 Australian republic referendum which was to amend the Constitution of Australia. The question asked whether to be a republic headed by the President or to retain the monarchy. As a reminder, the British monarch is Australia's sovereign and head of state.

Indigenous peoples

Colonialism caused the creation of a **reservation** system to keep **indigenous** peoples off of lands that Europeans wished to settle in. Even though, for some, it somehow allowed First Nations people to govern themselves and to maintain some of their cultural and social traditions, but, in the case of the Stolen generations, from 1910 onwards, far too many **Aboriginal** children were taken from their families to institutions to be trained and to be assimilated to Anglo-Australian culture.
Recently, the right of self-determination of indigenous peoples became a fundamental principle and has led to recent changes and apologies.
National commemoration days have been controversial whether it is in South Africa (Freedom Day) or New Zealand (Waitangi Day). Two relevant examples in Australia and in the United States shed light on the fact that celebrating the arrivals of the British is no longer welcome by the indigenous population.
For starters, Australia celebrates its national day on the 26 of January, but in recent years it has become an increasingly **heated** matter. It is suggested to change the date for it marks the landing of the first British **Fleet** in Sydney in 1788. For some, particularly the Aboriginals, it has become known as Invasion Day when the indigenous communities started to be oppressed and dispossessed of their lands. Similarly, in the United States, Indians contest Thanksgiving and Columbus Day as they consider them a **tribute** to the crimes of colonization. The second Monday of October celebrates the arrival of Christopher Columbus in 1492 in America. They have been asking for replacing Columbus Day by Indigenous People's Day. Some cities have already instituted to celebrate it as a counter-celebration held on the same day as the US federal holiday of Columbus Day.

Vocabulaire

Reservation an area dedicated to a tribe
Indigenous native
Aboriginal native
Heated controversial
Fleet group of ships
Tribute homage

Actualité

Australia has made progress in improving education for indigenous people, but is still falling short in many areas, a United Nations (UN) report has found.
Aboriginal Australians and Torres Strait Islanders, who together comprise 3% of the population, still experience high levels of disadvantage. Aboriginal people are massively overrepresented in the criminal justice system of Australia, more than 29% of the prison population is Aboriginal.

Exercices

01 Reading

THE STOLEN GENERATIONS

Between 1910 and the 1970s, many .... **[1]** children were forcibly removed from their families as a result of various governments .... **[2]**. The generations of children removed under these principles became known as the Stolen Generations. The policies of child removal left a .... **[3]** of trauma and loss that continues to affect Indigenous .... **[4]**, families and individuals today.

The forcible removal of Aboriginal and Torres Strait Islander children from their families was part of the policy of .... **[5]**, which was based on the misguided **assumption** that the lives of Aboriginal and Torres Strait Islander people would be improved if they became part of white society.

Policies focused on assimilating children as they were considered more adaptable to white society than adults. Children taken from their parents were taught to reject their Indigenous heritage and were forced to adopt white culture. Their names were often changed, and many were forbidden from speaking traditional languages. Some children were adopted by white families, and many were placed in institutions where abuse and neglect were common.

The Stolen Generations have had devastating impacts for the people who were forcibly removed as children, their parents and families, and their .... **[6]**. All three of these groups experience high rates of depression, anxiety, post-traumatic stress and suicide, and poor health and socioeconomic **outcomes**.

Individuals, families, communities and organisations (such as the Healing Foundation) have been working to reconnect members of the Stolen Generations and their descendants with family members, Indigenous communities, culture and country, and to heal the hurt caused by child .... **[7]**. Recommendations included financial .... **[8]** for victims of the Stolen Generations on a national level. Some state-level reparations have been made, however many people who were removed as children have found they don't fit the criteria for these compensation schemes. Others have said that no amount of money will ever be able to compensate them for the trauma they were put through.

Adapted from www.australianstogether.or.au
Source: https://australianstogether.org.au/discover/australian-history/stolen-generations

A) Complete the text with the following words.

a) policies
b) descendants
c) compensation
d) communities
e) removals
f) First Nations
g) legacy
h) assimilation

Wordbox
Assumption idea
Outcomes results

B) Put the main ideas of the text in the right order.

a) The principle of the policy.
b) The generations of children removed from their families are called the Stolen generations.
c) The compensation.
d) The assimilation of children.
e) The impacts of the policy.

02 Civilization

Match the word with the definition.

1. The American Dream
2. The First Amendment
3. The War of Independence
4. The Pilgrim Fathers
5. The Founding Fathers
6. Rag to riches
7. A self-made man
8. The Cold War
9. Rockefeller
10. Puritan

a) Upward social mobility.
b) The belief that every American can be successful with hard work.
c) The element of the Constitution that guarantees Free Speech.
d) The period of political tensions between the Soviet Union and the United States.
e) The originators of the Constitution.
f) The revolutionary war of the 13 colonies and Britain.
g) A famous rich businessman.
h) The first settlers.
i) Someone who believes in hard work, in the protestant tradition.
j) An independently successful man.

Equalities and inequalities

Égalités et inégalités

Social segregation

Today, there is **undeniably** still a lack of access to social goods such as education, healthcare and housing, that is brought about by discrimination linked to religion, prestige, race, ethnicity, gender, age, sexual orientation, and class. Social inequality usually implies the lack of equality of **wages** but it may alternatively be conceptualized in terms of the lack of equality of access to opportunity.

Inequality can be reduced by **implementing** institutional arrangements on the field of fiscal, social, and economic policy. In countries that have a universal health care system, health inequalities have been reduced. In Canada, for example, equity in the availability of health services has been improved dramatically through Medicare (since 1966), similarly to Medicaid (since 1965) and Obamacare (since 2010) in the United States. Besides, improving access to roads, communications and markets can have a great impact on reducing regional inequality.

Social class

Social mobility refers to the shift in an individual's social status from one status to another: upward or downward mobility is when a person moves from a lower position in society to a higher one or vice versa.

Some social groups are **clustered**. We face a social paralysis that questions societal shift and solidarity.

Class distinctions are a central element of British life, especially compared to a country like the United States where hard-work and ambition are viewed as the only limits. TV shows such as *Downtown Abbey* and *Upstairs, Downstairs* illustrate these distinctions. The issue **lies** in the fact that it is difficult to move from one to another and society doesn't make it easy for classes to interact. Today, the elite still **possesses** institutional authority though social mobility has increased with improvements in education and **social welfare**.

The class of origin remains an important factor in recruitment to higher status occupations. People who can afford attending **top-rated** universities like Oxford and Cambridge will be more likely to occupy a higher social status. The highest ranked universities gather into coalitions such as the Russell Group in the United Kingdom, and the Group of Eight in Australia, the Ivy League in the United States.

Caste system

For generations of Indians, the ancient code of social stratification known as the **caste** system has defined how people earn a living, where they live, what they eat and who they marry. At birth, every child inherits his or her ancestor's caste which determines their social status. As the highest

Vocabulaire

- **Undeniably** without doubt
- **Wages** salaries
- **Implementing** applying
- **Clustered** aggregated
- **Lies** is
- **Possesses** owns
- **Social welfare** government benefits
- **Top-rated** highly regarded
- **Caste** social class

of all the castes, and traditionally priests or teachers, Brahmins make up a small part of the Indian population. An entire population in India and Hindu regions of Nepal, Sri Lanka, is often considered below the class system: the "Untouchables", who now are more often known as Dalits and perceived as the lowest of the low.
In 1948, negative discrimination on the basis of caste was banned by law and further **enshrined** in the Indian Constitution; however, the system continues to be practiced in India with devastating social effects. The caste system in India is today the basis of a stratified society which justifies discrimination and inequality.

Women

Before the emancipation of women, men held all the resources, they could decide anything about their **spouse**'s life, namely their education. Women were banned from universities. They progressively thought they deserve to be emancipated from their enslaved status. For hundreds of years women have worked for their emancipation **enforcing** the right to vote and to earn a living. Feminism has been **striving** to liberate women from the traditional power structures, to eliminate gender discrimination from laws, and define legal standards to foster their full equality with men. It has led to the redistribution of roles in the family.
Nevertheless, equality of men and women is not to be taken for granted, nor is it universal even today. In many parts of the world, women are unable to move freely. The media contribute to denounce that women are still victims of the gender pay gap. While most women effectively earn less than men today, they still support most of the house chores. Affirmative action contributes to **shatter** the **glass ceiling** or as *All-Women Shortlists*, an action to increase women's presence in politics in Britain.

Discrimination

Other types of discrimination can be based on sexual orientation, disability or ethnicity, among others. In the United States, sexual orientation discrimination – whether gay, lesbian, bisexual, or heterosexual – is illegal in public and private workplaces as a result of a 2020 Supreme Court decision. To fight against social prejudice against people with disabilities, as called ableism or disablism, the Rehabilitation Act of 1973 enacted into law certain civil penalties for failing to make public places comply with access codes.
There are culturally acceptable terms of racial abuse in the United States: redneck and WASP (White Anglo-Saxon Protestant). Both refer to descendants of the English Protestant settlers. Hollywood is authorised to portray rednecks as generally rural whites and WASPs as an elite.
White supremacists have been depicted in films and documentaries, showing for example the actions of the Ku Klux Klan. Today, the anonymity which the Internet provides can make it difficult to track the extent of their violence, leading to an increase in the amount of hate crimes.

Vocabulaire

Enshrined consecrated
Spouse wife
Enforcing imposing
Striving struggling
Shatter break into pieces
Glass ceiling limit to raise in work hierarchy

Actualité

Black Lives Matter is a movement protesting against racially motivated violence against black people including incidents of police brutality. It all started in 2013. The movement began with the use of the hashtag #BlackLivesMatter to denounce George Zimmerman's hate crime on African-American teen Trayvon Martin.
In 2020, the movement returned to the headlines during the global George Floyd protests, following the killing of George Floyd by a policeman. The movement gained international attention and is one of the largest movement in the country's history.

Exercices

01 Civilization

Watch this video and answer the following questions.

Title : Upstairs, Downstairs, Series 2

https://www.youtube.com/watch?v=ThYZL3d0c9w

1) What type of document is it?
- ❑ **a.** A teaser
- ❑ **b.** A trailer

2) Where is it situated?
- ❑ **a.** London
- ❑ **b.** New York City

3) Where do the protagonists take their meals?
- ❑ **a.** In the same place
- ❑ **b.** At separate tables

4) What is the address?
- ❑ **a.** 165 Eaton Palace
- ❑ **b.** 165 Eaton Place

5) When is it happening?
- ❑ **a.** World War I
- ❑ **b.** World War II

6) What is the status of the Indian character Amanjit Singh?
- ❑ **a.** He is one of the servants
- ❑ **b.** He is a member of the family

7) Why does Amanjit Singh get mad?
- ❑ **a.** Indians served in the army to fight for the British
- ❑ **b.** Indians have to serve in the army to fight for the British

8) What is the show entitled *Upstairs, Downstairs*, according to you?
- ❑ **a.** It talks about social class
- ❑ **b.** It is the outbreak of war

9) What is upward mobility?
- ❑ **a.** To lower of one's social class
- ❑ **b.** To rise to a higher social position

10) What is the Russell group?
- ❑ **a.** An association of the best universities in the United Kingdom
- ❑ **b.** An association of the best universities in Australia

02 Vocabulary

Fill in the crossword.

Horizontal

3) move from a position in society to another one
4) a group of top-ranked British universities
5) enfranchisement
7) a law that allows suffrage
9) medical services
12) separation
14) the lowest cast in India
15) the difference in salary between men and women

Vertical

1) intolerance
2) salaries
6) the highest caste in India
8) an English top-rated university
10) equality
11) the name of social classes in India
13) healthcare program launched by Obama

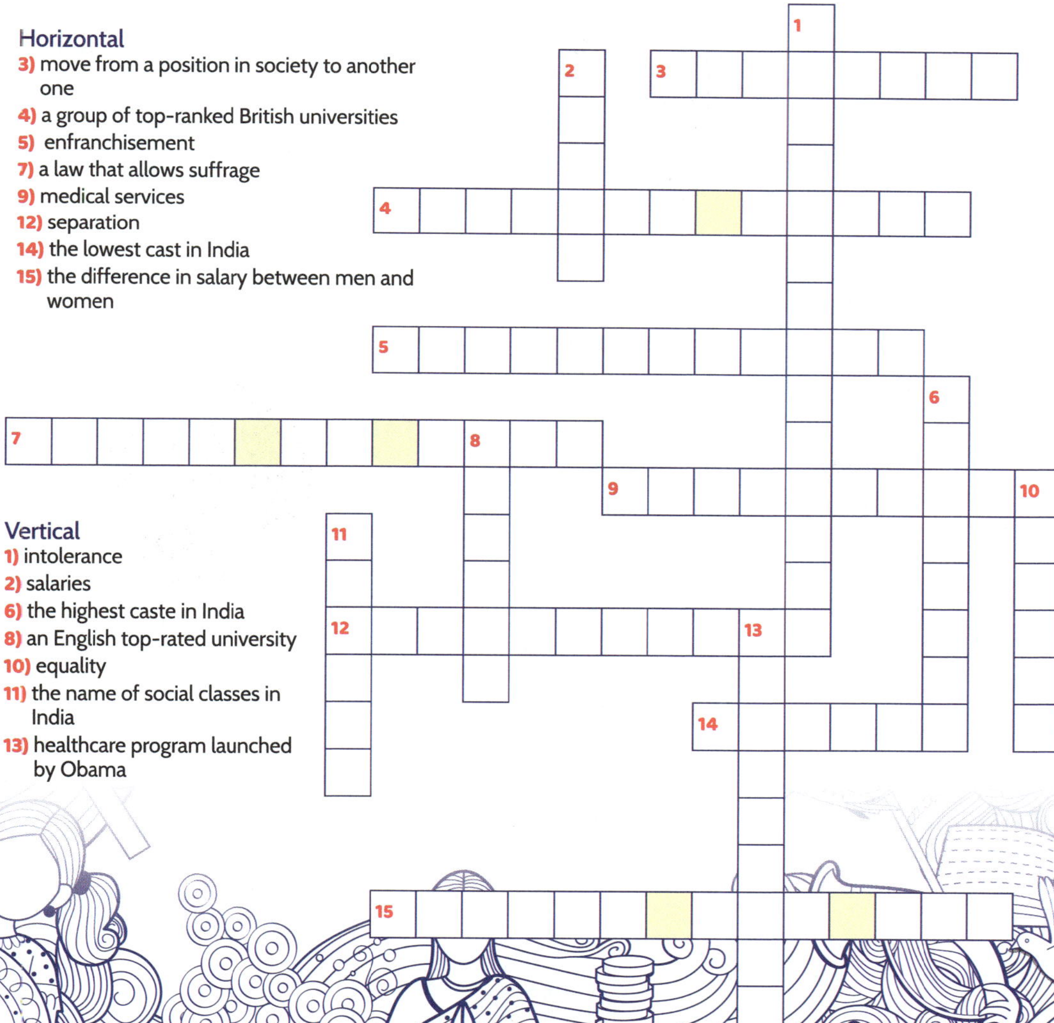

Synthesis: Unity and plurality

Unity in plurality

- Many diasporas in English-speaking countries are either a source of renewal or creating a lack of unity
- Plurality as multiculturalism contributes to unity

From the melting-pot to the salad bowl

- American identity is centered upon the melting-pot
- The Statue of Liberty's poem
- Minorities' fight for their rights
- The emergence of the salad bowl

Unity and plurality

Language

- Language defines national identity and participates in integration
- Language register or accent in English and social class

Separatism

- The impact of language is also on the support for separatism, like in Wales for example
- Language is a tool for domination, such as in South Africa

Religion

- Some English-speaking countries have various religious conflicts
- The Kashmir conflict between India and Pakistan
- The conflict between protestants and catholics in Ireland

Synthesis: Public liberties and individual liberties

Public liberties and individual liberties

The land of freedom

- The United States is a model of freedom: the Pilgrim Fathers, the Founding Fathers
- The American Dream of the self-made man

Freedom of speech

- The United States' strong freedom of speech given by the First Amendment
- Restrictions to the First Amendment by pro-life activists, political-correctness fundamentalists or white supremacists

Individual liberties

- In the 1960s, in the United Kingdom, fertility control became more widespread
- In 1967, the Abortion Act made abortion legal
- In 2015, in the Republic of Ireland, the campaign #HomeToVote, to vote for same-sex marriage

Separatism

- Federations and unions have not always been accepted, leading to separatism
- Examples in Quebec, Wales, Northern Ireland, and Scotland
- The Australian republic referendum to end the monarchy

Indigenous peoples

- Colonialism caused the creation of reservations
- Example of the Stolen generations in Australia
- Controversy about commemoration days that celebrate the invasion of indigenous lands
- The national day in Australia
- Thanksgiving and Columbus Day in the United States

Synthesis: Equalities and inequalities

Social segregation

- A lack of access to social goods because of discrimination
- Inequality can be reduced with measures
- Healthcare programs: Medicare, Medicaid, Obamacare

Social class

- Social mobility can be paralyzed
- Social class is an element of Britishness
- Social class defines occupations and education

Equalities and inequalities

Discriminations

- In the United States, sexual orientation discrimination is illegal since 2020
- Racial abuse via acceptable vocabulary: redneck and WASP
- White supremacists' actions have been depicted in films and have increased with the Internet

Women

- Gradual emancipation of women
- Efforts are still to be made to reach equity between men and women, namely to end the gender pay gap
- Affirmative action reduces the glass ceiling and increases women's presence in politics

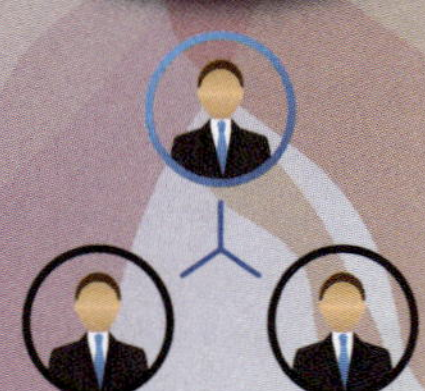

Caste system

- The caste system defines people's social status
- From Brahmins to Dalits
- Ban of discrimination on the basis of caste but still effective today

☐ Première

☑ Terminale

Changing environments

Environnements en mutation

- **Frontier and space**

  Frontière et espace

- **From the protection of nature to ecological transition**

  De la protection de la nature à la transition écologique

- **Rethink the city**

  Repenser la ville

Frontier and space

Frontière et espace

Frontiers

The idea of frontier applies to tourism and the subsequent preservation of distinctive sites such as Cliffs of Moher in Ireland, the Great Barrier Reef in Australia, or Lake Powell, Monument Valley and Canyon Chelly in the United States as well as the Hawaiian archipelago.
However, in the course of history, the opening and the closing of frontiers generated a lot of tensions.
As a case in point, the idea of frontier has **forged** the country. The conception of Britain as an insular nation is also a myth, **albeit** one of the central myths of British history. After World War II, a worldwide process of decolonization began in which Britain **granted** independence to all of its major colonies. From the independence of India to the handover of Hong Kong, the British Empire has dealt with insurgencies and revolts in the various places.
The Irish **border** is a striking example of perpetual tension about sovereignty. In 1922, the Republic of Ireland **seceded** from the United Kingdom as a self-governing dominion, setting the stage for full national independence, while Northern Ireland remained part of the United Kingdom.
As the Republic of Ireland is still a member of the European Union after Brexit, the border between the Republic of Ireland and Northern Ireland is becoming the only external European Union land border between the United Kingdom and the European Union.

The Frontier Myth

The Frontier Myth is the oldest American national myth and has shaped the American identity. The myth recognizes that the United States developed as a settler state, which grew geographically and increased in political and economic power by advancing European settlements into the territory of Native Americans. Manifest Destiny, a phrase **coined** in 1845, is the idea that the United States is destined to expand its dominion and spread democracy and capitalism across the entire North American continent. The idea of individualism, self-reliance and heroism are **embedded** in the myth, as well as the idea that the progress of a nation was obtained by violence.
The idea of New Frontier was coined by John Fitzgerald Kennedy in his program to **tackle** economic and social issues and to continue to move forward with the space conquest. Kennedy challenged the American people and government to put a man on the moon by the end of the decade.
Over the last fifty years, various missions to Mars have sought to determine the probability of life. Today, people see the red planet as the Last Frontier, which brings about a lot of fiction works.

Vocabulaire

Forged shaped
Albeit although
Granted gave
Border frontier
Seceded separated
Coined created
Embedded rooted
Tackle deal with

Migrations

Globalization has been profitable for many developing countries. Protectionism, unfair working conditions, exploitation of labor have led to social injustice. The richest 20 percent of the world's population consume 86 percent of the world's resources while the poorest 80 percent consume just 14 percent. That is why, more and more countries are experiencing significant volumes of migrations.

Free trade reduces barriers between nations and promotes global economic growth. **Labor** can move from country to country to market their skills. It has the potential to make this world a better place to live in and solve some of the deep problems like unemployment and poverty.

In the United States, the Sun Belt is the southern area of the country from North Carolina to California. It has seen a substantial population growth since the 1960s. The migration to the Sun Belt from the North-East's manufacturing Rust Belt is a phenomenon of an entire generation in search of new opportunities in a sunnier environment. It is a reminder of the Founding Fathers' **pledge** of the pursuit of happiness.

South Americans are willing to take their chance and get into the United States illegally to make ends meet and earn a living wage for their family back home. A day's work in the United States is worth twice or three times as much as what a Mexican would do south of the border. The 2,000 miles United States-Mexican border patrols are overwhelmed for the border is **porous**. "Wetbacks" risk to be fatally injured crossing the border: they swim across rivers, but they also scale or gate-crash fences, or sneak into the desert.

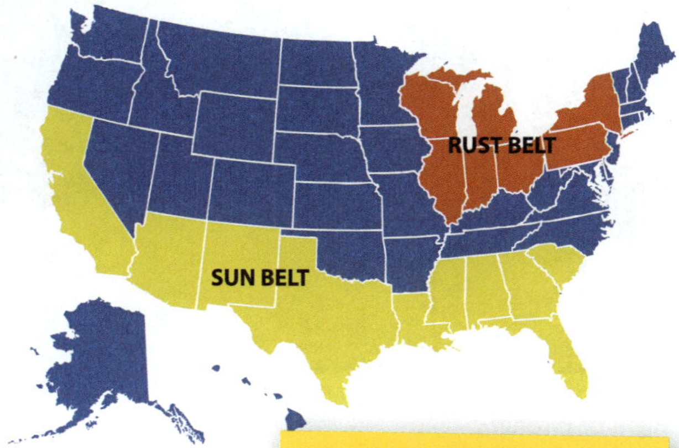

Virtual expansion

The digital world is an open world and is a convenient way of knowing the news or current events. In a more global aspect, it has contributed to **bridge** the **digital divide** by making it possible to more users to have access to information and knowledge.

In recent years, role-playing games is gaining in popularity and online streaming platforms are emerging.

Having a social media account is a part of today's society. People create a personal virtual space and use it to connect to others, build relationships with individuals who have similar interests, to share and comment on anything they find interesting.

Vocabulaire

Free trade policy with no restrictions on imports and exports between countries

Labor workforce

Pledge promise

Porous permeable

Bridge overcome

Digital divide the gap between people who have access to computers and the Internet and people who do not

Actualité

Borders have always played a symbolic and political function in times of crisis. Border closures as well as containment measures decided by a vast number of countries with the view of limiting the spread of COVID-19 has had a dire impact on the global economy. Travel restrictions left many travellers stranded in foreign countries and contributed to an unprecedented drop-off in global travel. The COVID pandemic is a crisis without borders.

Exercices

01 Civilization

Fence separating the United States and Mexico.

Right or Wrong?

1) The snapshot depicts a border. ○ Right ○ Wrong

2) The picture conveys the idea of shortness. ○ Right ○ Wrong

3) The US-Mexican border is 1,000 miles long. ○ Right ○ Wrong

4) South Americans immigrate to the United States for financial reasons. ○ Right ○ Wrong

5) Immigrants are called "wetbacks" because they swim across the river to cross the border. ○ Right ○ Wrong

6) Americans migrate to the Sun Belt in search of sun and happiness. ○ Right ○ Wrong

7) Detroit and Chicago are situated in the Sun Belt. ○ Right ○ Wrong

8) The name Rust Belt derives from its industrial decline. ○ Right ○ Wrong

9) The Founding Fathers are the first settlers on American soil. ○ Right ○ Wrong

10) The Founding Fathers' pledge is "liberty, life, the pursuit of happiness". ○ Right ○ Wrong

02 Culture

Match the picture with the tourist site.

1. Canyon Chelly, USA
2. Monument Valley, USA
3. Hawaiian archipelago, USA
4. Lake Powell, USA
5. Niagara Falls, Canada
6. Stonehenge, England
7. The Giant's Causeway, Northern Ireland
8. The Outback, Australia
9. Great Barrier Reef, Australia
10. Cliffs of Moher, Ireland

03 Language

Translate these sentences into English.

a) Les technologies numériques ont profondément transformé la relation entre les individus.

....

....

b) Depuis l'émergence des réseaux sociaux, rester en contact avec des parents est devenu aisé.

....

....

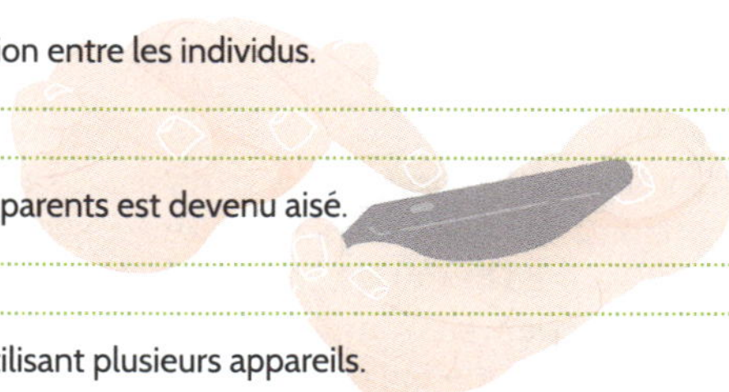

c) Aujourd'hui, on peut publier des informations et communiquer en utilisant plusieurs appareils.

....

....

d) Un des avantages évident des réseaux sociaux est qu'on peut immédiatement joindre les gens de n'importe où.

....

....

e) Internet contribue à réduire la fracture numérique en donnant l'accès à l'information et à la connaissance.

....

....

From the protection of nature to ecological transition

De la protection de la nature à la transition écologique

Industrialization

The world's modern environmental problems began or were greatly exacerbated by the Industrial Revolution and mass-consumption. It has led to an increased **reliance** on **fossil fuels** i.e. coal, oil, and gas to power farm machinery and to produce fertilizers and pesticides. These fossil fuels are the dominant source of local air pollution and emitter of carbon dioxide and **greenhouse gases**. The need for labor initiated urbanization with migrations to cities that were ill-prepared to handle them.

Besides, the use of natural resources throughout human society leads to environmental changes. Converting forests to mostly paved urban areas changed the rivers and the water infiltration.

The amount of valuable natural resources reduced because natural resources such as water, trees, soil, rocks and minerals, wild and domesticated animals were transformed for production.

To sum up, the more countries industrialize in pursuit of their own **wealth**, the greater this ecological transformation becomes.

Ideologies

According to the **First Nations**, nature is sacred and has to be protected. In Australia, the Aboriginal culture is based on a spiritual relationship between humans, animals, plants and the Earth. It was during what has become known as the Dreamtime, that the land, mountains, hills, rivers, plants, life forms both animal and human and the sky above were formed by the actions of supernatural spirits. In the United States, the indigenous culture is founded on the respect of the Great Spirit called Wakan Tanka that is the sacredness that resides in everything in Mother Nature.

A spiritual movement called New Age rapidly grew in the Western world during the 1970s at which time it was centered largely in the United Kingdom. It expanded and grew largely in the 1980s and 1990s, in particular within the United States. The counterculture of the 1960s and the anti-consumerist hippie culture exerted a strong influence on the early development of various ecologist movements such as New Age.

Vocabulaire

- **Reliance** dependence
- **Fossil fuels** fuels from organic remains
- **Greenhouse gases** gases causing global warming
- **Wealth** richness
- **First Nations** first peoples

Natural resources management

Managing natural resources is a matter of great importance, both politically, socially, environmentally and economically.

It is important to regulate the **stream flow** of rivers such as the Mississippi river and the Colorado river in the United States, the Saint Lawrence river in Canada, the Murray-Darling basin in Australia, and the Thames in England. The impacts of climate change also interact with land management and landscape preservation as well as the existing problems of overfishing in Canada and Scotland.

There are environmental concerns in relation to **shale gas** extraction and oil **drilling** in Arctic and Alaska. Oil companies are one-step closer to drilling on the coastal plain of Alaska's Arctic National Wildlife Refuge: the land is home to polar bears and caribou, and part of the migratory route for snow geese. The machinery and equipment that workers use for drilling oil release an **array** of harmful air pollutants.

Crisis

We have to be aware that some of the deadliest disasters are man-made. Those tsunamis, earthquakes, hurricanes, and typhoons are nothing more than a reaction to our actions. Everyone is responsible for the global challenges of the food **shortage**, loss of biodiversity, the extinction of species and widespread air and water pollution. Major current environmental issues also include climate changes with **heat waves**, **drought** and **floods**.

Bush fire seasons in California or in Australia are linked to global warming as record heat and dry conditions usually precedes the **outbreak**.

The unprecedented Australian bushfire season, also known as the Black Summer, started in June 2019, in the two territories situated in the north: the Northern Territory and Queensland. Then fires heavily impacted various regions of the eastern states of New South Wales and Victoria, the smallest and most southern state. By March 2020, the last fire of the season occurred in Western Australia.

In 2020, California faced the largest fire season in its history triggering mass evacuations. The intensity has been attributed to poor forest management and a combination of a record-breaking heat wave and strong winds.

Tackling the impact of climate change and facilitating a just ecological transition is a priority. The world must balance the role of energy in development with the need to transition towards renewable-energy resources and reduce the generation of greenhouse gases.

Vocabulaire

- **Stream flow** the current of a river
- **Shale gas** gas from rocks
- **Drilling** make a hole
- **Array** variety
- **Shortage** scarcity
- **Heat waves** a period of hot weather
- **Drought** a period of lack of water
- **Floods** an overflow of water
- **Bush fire** wildfire
- **Outbreak** beginning

Actualité

The Paris Agreement was signed during the Paris Climate Conference by the COP 21 in 2015. Ratified by 197 countries, including the United States, it is the first global treaty to explicitly address climate change. However, the international cooperation has been affected by government alternation. Whereas President Obama marked an historic moment in the global efforts to combat climate change, by signing the Paris Agreement in 2015, as soon as President Trump took office, the United States withdrew from the Agreement. Now, more recently, hours after he was sworn in, President Biden announced that the United States plans to reenter the Agreement.

Exercices

01 Reading

HEAVY RAINS FLOOD PARTS OF NEW DELHI, TRIGGERING CHAOS

Heavy .... [1] rains have flooded parts of India's capital New Delhi and its suburbs, throwing life out of **gear** for millions of people, as the death **toll** from the annual deluge across South Asia rose to nearly 1,300.

In New Delhi's suburb of Gurgaon, **dubbed** the Millenium City, roads, underpasses and residential areas were flooded on Wednesday forcing power cuts in several areas. Rafts were put into action to evacuate people in some areas.

The monsoon is vital to the densely populated region, revitalizing .... [2] and waterways amid **scorching** summers. But it also causes widespread death and destruction.

In New Delhi, commuters battled through **knee-deep** waters and cars and buses were submerged as torrential .... [3] added to traffic **woes** in the city of 20 million.

At a museum in Jaipur in the mostly .... [4] state of Rajasthan, staff told AFP how they were forced to smash open a glass display case containing a 2,300-year-old Egyptian mummy in order to save it from rainwater flooding the ground floor.

The torrid conditions in recent days also hit India's northern and eastern states. In India's poorest state, Bihar, eight million people have been hit by the .... [5], with thousands of displaced people sleeping on embankments and highways amid a .... [6] of relief camps.

This year's rains have also come in the wake of the economic devastation **wrought** by the coronavirus pandemic, with the loss of .... [7] across flood-affected areas a further blow to farmers and rural communities.

More than six million people have had their homes damaged by the floods, and tens of thousands of villagers remain in shelters. Others are sleeping in huts built on roads on higher ground, unable to return to their submerged homes.

Nepal's monsoon toll tops 200 for most years, but experts say this year's .... [8] have been particularly deadly due to the continuing after-effects of the massive 2015 .... [9] and more road construction in the country's Himalayan .... [10].

Adapted from www.aljazeera.com, 20 January 2020
Source: https://www.aljazeera.com/news/2020/08/heavy-rains-flood-parts-delhi-triggering-chaos-200820043257651.html

A) **Complete the text with the following words.**

a) monsoon
b) desert
c) rains
d) land
e) shortage
f) floods
g) earthquakes
h) landslides
i) foothills
j) crops

Wordbox

Gear order
Toll number
Dubbed named
Scorching burning
Knee-deep as high as the knees
Woes difficulties
Wrought shaped

02 Vocabulary

A) **Complete the map with the main territories.**

1) **Western Australia** is the western state.
2) **Northern Territory** is the land of Uluru.
3) Adelaide is the capital of the state of **South Australia**.
4) The Great Barrier Reef is off the coast of **Queensland**.
5) Canberra and Sydney are located in **New South Wales**.
6) **Victoria** is the small southernest state.
7) **Tasmania** is an island state.

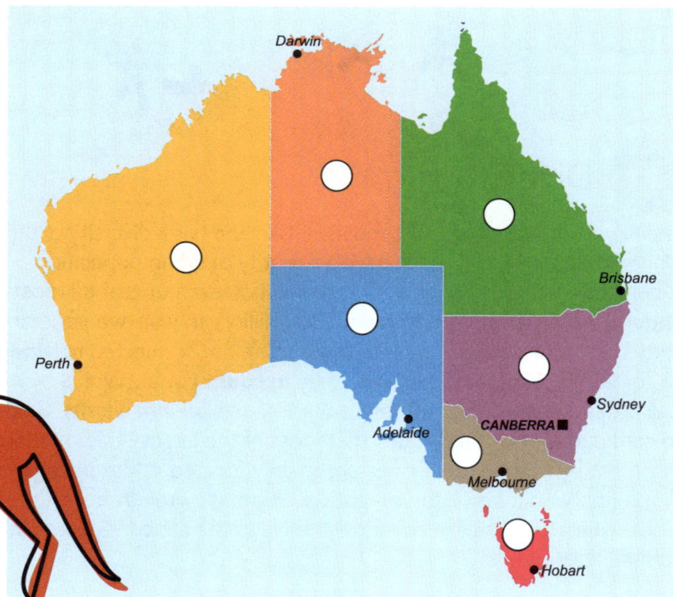

B) **Associate two words to create a compound noun.**

1 fossil ○
2 natural ○
3 bush ○
4 climate ○
5 land ○
6 oil ○
7 food ○
8 heat ○
9 global ○
10 greenhouse ○

○ change a
○ drilling b
○ waves c
○ shortage d
○ gases e
○ warming f
○ fires g
○ fuels h
○ resources i
○ preservation j

Diversity

The English-speaking world is mostly urban and has a diversity of urban models. Australia, the United States, the United Kingdom and Canada have a majority of urban population.
Nigeria comprises 50% of city residents, however, one of its most sprawling city, Lagos, grew 100-fold, from under 200 000 people to nearly 20 million, in just two generations. There, most residents live in informal settlements, or slums. The great majority are not connected to **piped** water or a sanitation system.
As for Kenya, India, and Tanzania, they **account for** a majority of rural population. In India, Delhi, Mumbai and Calcutta are megacities with more than 10 million inhabitants. Globally, the number of megacities is projected to continue to rise. It illustrates that most of the largest cities are located in the less developed countries, while the most powerful global cities are mainly located in the developed countries. It is common to separate the demographic nature of the megacities' dramatic growth from the specific economic dimension of the rise of global cities. Cities such as London and New York are considered global cities mainly for economic, political and cultural reasons.

Supercities

The concept of megalopolis has become highly influential as it introduces a new, larger scale in thinking about urban growth. As a case point, California's major urban areas were **coined** the name *SanSan* as an allusion to San Diego, in the south, and San Francisco, in the north. Similarly, *BosWash* refers to the supercity that spreads from Boston to Washington, as well as *ChiPitts*, from Chicago to Pittsburg.
In California, the major increase in wealth in San Francisco has been attributed with the **dot-com** boom in the 1990s, creating a strong demand for countless skilled tech workers from local startups and close by Silicon Valley businesses leading to rising standards of living. As a result, a large influx of new workers in the Internet and technology sector began to contribute to the **gentrification** of historically poor immigrant neighborhoods.

Vocabulaire

Piped running
Account for is composed of
Coined nicknamed
Dot-com tech companies
Gentrification renewal including the displacement of low-income residents

Spatial inequalities

Spatial inequalities imply the development over time of distinct areas of urban **deprivation**. In the United States, gated communities provide the perception of security and exclusivity but show that social cohesion and urban public spaces are in crisis. On the contrary, ghettos are often known for being more impoverished than other areas of the city. Buying or renting a house in a predominantly white neighborhood is often expensive and whites are willing to pay to live in these gated communities. As urban population increases, so does segregation. In other words, larger cities are more segregated than smaller ones.
In South Africa, from the late 19th century until the end of apartheid, some urban areas were reserved for non-whites. Today, these townships such as Soweto are still underdeveloped, racially segregated urban areas.

Gentrification

The gentrification of city suburbs implies a considerable increase in rents and is destroying communities.
Among disadvantaged groups in Australia's largest cities, the situation of First Nations proves that they are involved in rural-to-urban migration with the presence of enclaves, in the form of areas of low socio-economic status.
The 1950s policy of assimilation forced significant Indigenous migration from the **bush** to towns and cities and was essentially an experiment to force Indigenous people to give up their beliefs and traditions as they adapted to urban life. Today, in parts of cities such as Brisbane, Melbourne and Sydney, we find the continued presence of an urban Aboriginal community.
Yet the place of Indigenous in Australia's cities is under threat. The **dispersal** that began with European invasion continues through the gentrification of city suburbs where Indigenous identities persist. They are being displaced again. Faced with rapid housing price increases, urban Indigenous populations continue to relocate to the outer suburbs, where cheaper housing is usually located. Some say it is a new form of dispersal, forced by capitalistic motive that perpetuates the cycle of Aboriginal disadvantage.

Urban design

As the world urbanises, new urban practices are developing to better design everything from offices to streets to transport. Ecodistricts are designed to integrate objectives of sustainable development and social equity and contribute to reduce the ecological footprint of an area.
The emergence of electric bikes and the expansion of cycling infrastructure in cities have been one of the great global urban success stories of the century. Urban planning is aiming to closing streets to cars and making the most of the local streetscape by turning them green and parklike.
Smart cities are constructed to optimize the efficiency of city operations and services and connect to citizens. The buildings have automatic climate control and computerized access; the roads are embedded with electronic sensors to enable the city's brain to respond to the movement of residents and to manage urban flows.

Vocabulaire

Deprivation shortage
Bush Australian savana
Dispersal scattering

Actualité

In 2020, the faces of US cities have been forever altered by the pandemic. In fact, millions of Americans fled big cities to escape the coronavirus pandemic and many of them are staying permanently. Thanks to the remote working possibilities, they can move away and have access to more affordable homes. They want greener surroundings and wide-open spaces. Those who haven't been lucky enough to escape urban sprawl are undoubtedly yearning for more space.

Exercices

01 Civilization

Watch this video and answer the questions.

Source : Chicago Council on global affairs

https://www.youtube.com/watch?v=2x8zmA9RYrM&ab_channel=ChicagoCouncilonGlobalAffairs

1) Why is the overall message of the video?
- ❑ **a.** The message is to inform about the issue of global cities
- ❑ **b.** The message is to promote the city of Chicago

2) How many people reside in 60 global cities?
- ❑ **a.** Nearly 1 million people reside in 60 global cities
- ❑ **b.** Nearly 1 billion people reside in 60 global cities

3) What is the first feature of a global city?
- ❑ **a.** Global cities are economic powerhouses
- ❑ **b.** Global cities reward celebrities

4) What is the second characteristic?
- ❑ **a.** Infrastructures
- ❑ **b.** Business

5) What is the Bean?
- ❑ **a.** A monument in Chicago
- ❑ **b.** The metro in Chicago

6) What is the third characteristic?
- ❑ **a.** Conferences
- ❑ **b.** Knowledge

7) What is the fourth one?
- ❑ **a.** Culture
- ❑ **b.** Entertainment

8) What is the fifth one?
- ❑ **a.** Politics
- ❑ **b.** Climate

9) What does "think globally" mean?
- ❑ **a.** It means that business, ideas and people flow freely
- ❑ **b.** It means to understand the importance of connecting local politics to global politics

10) Finally, what is the last characteristic?
- ❑ **a.** Openness
- ❑ **b.** Museums

02 Language

A) Separate the words with a dash.

diversityurbanpopulationcityslumscountriesmegalopolisstartupsgentrificationghettotownship

B) Classify the words in two columns: adjectives and nouns.

a development
b spatial
c distinct
d areas
e inequalities
f urban
g gated
h deprivation
i communities
j cohesion
k impoverished
l segregated
m social
n apartheid
o underdeveloped

Adjectives	Nouns

C) Find as many words as you can by matching the two parts.

Consider- Work- Power- Count-

Busi- Most- Neighbor-

-ABLE -ER -FUL -LESS -NESS -LY -HOOD

Synthesis: Frontier and space

The Frontier Myth

- The Frontier Myth, the oldest American national myth
- Manifest Destiny justifies the expansion and the spreading of democracy and capitalism
- JFK's New Frontier: a social and space program
- Today's Last Frontier: Mars

Migrations

- Globalization and free trade have a positive impact. But causes inequities hence migrations
- The migration to the Sun Belt in the United States, in pursuit of happiness
- The immigration of South Americans in the United States

Frontier and space

Virtual expansion

- The digital world is an open world and makes it possible to bridge the digital divide
- The rise of role-playing games and online streaming platforms
- Social media to connect to each other

Frontiers

- Tourism and the preservation of sites
- Frontier means tensions
- Britain's insularity is a myth
- Decolonization of the British Empire
- The Irish border: a continual conflict and the consequences of Brexit

Synthesis: From the protection of nature to ecological transition

Industrialization

- Environmental problems due to the Industrial Revolution and mass-consumption
- Human society's dependence on energy and use of resources

Ideologies

- The First nations consider nature as sacred such as in Australia and the United States
- New age and other ecologist movements

From the protection of nature to ecological transition

Natural resources management

- Managing natural resources is important
- Water and land management
- Overfishing
- Shale gas extraction and oil drilling

Crisis

- A large number of man-made disasters
- Bush fires in Australia
- Ecological transition is a priority

Synthesis: Rethink the city

Diversity

- The English-speaking world is mostly urban
- A diversity of urban models: megacities with more than 10 million inhabitants is increasing
- The rise of Global cities

Supercities

- Megalopolis are major urban areas: SanSan, BosWash, ChiPitts
- San Francisco' Silicon Valley expansion with the dot-com boom
- Subsequent gentrification of poor neighborhood

Rethink the city

Spatial inequalities

- Gentrification due to housing prices
- In the 1950s, Aboriginal rural-to-urban migration
- Today, migration to outer suburbs for economic reasons

Urban design

- New urban practices are developing such as ecodistricts
- Cycling infrastructures are expanding
- Smart cities optimizes city operations and manages urban flows

☐ Première

☑ Terminale

Relation with the world

Relation au monde

- **Power and influence**
  Puissance et influence
- **Rivalries and interdependences**
  Rivalités et interdépendances
- **Common heritage and diversity**
  Héritage commun et diversité

Power and influence

Puissance et influence

Imperialism

The concepts of power and influence are at the heart of international relations.
The relations between the countries of the English-speaking world have **unfolded** from settlement and domination to cooperation. The British Empire imposed its rule and stood as a world leader. The English-speaking world remains very influential in various fields including economy, politics and culture.
The decolonization of the British Empire that started with the independence of India in 1948 has lowered the influence of the United Kingdom and lead to the rise of American hegemony.
The development of globalization is often viewed as a new form of western hegemony over developing countries and American imperialism has shown its limits.
For a very long time, the United States was an **unrivaled** superpower which **exerted** influence or projected power on a global scale and showed the way to other countries. However, today, other superpowers such as India and China are emerging.
The two business districts Wall Street and the City of London have become the great symbols of wealth and power. New York City's financial industry became centered on Wall Street. It is an economic engine which is home to the world's two largest stock exchanges.

The BBC

Headquartered in London, the BBC, British Broadcasting Corporation, is the world's oldest national broadcaster across radio, TV and the Internet. The BBC has played a prominent role in British life and culture and has been an effective instrument of soft power. The BBC's high reputation globally is based on preventing misinformation and the widespread dissemination of fake news with various platforms used for fact checking. The BBC is a global brand: its journalism reach audiences around the world.
For decades, it has been the face and voice of Britain overseas. Its attraction and influence abroad remain strong, but is **on the wane**, reflecting the United Kingdom's declining economic and political position on the world stage.
Many foreign governments complain about partiality. As an illustration, the relationship between the BBC and Indian listeners was damaged because it represented the voice of a colonial empire. Even after the independence, a **bias** against India was discernable in BBC broadcasts in particular concerning the conflict with Pakistan. In the 1970s, the BBC was **expelled** from India by order of Gandhi to limit British neo-imperialism.

Vocabulaire

Unfolded happened
Unrivaled having no equal
Exerted used
On the wane in decline
Bias partiality
Expelled excluded

Global village

At the beginning of the 20th century, America's soft power first began by exporting some of its home-grown culture abroad through films and music e.g. Charlie Chaplin and Westerns became familiar to millions outside the country. The Americanization of the world continued with the rise of the consumer society and the American lifestyle in the 1950s which had a deep impact on the world.
This American mode of domination is non-territorial and, thus, is distinct from the European powers: Americans are globalizing at the same time as they are americanizing the world.
Today's worldwide dominance of CNN in the media, Hollywood in the entertainment industry or McDonald's **epitomizes** a US-influenced global village. Americans have made Hollywood their dream factory and the rest of the world **has followed suit**. Much of the 20th century culture will be remembered worldwide through the films made in Hollywood, thanks to the talent of numerous filmmakers. The studios were set in the neighborhood of Hollywood in Los Angeles, a **real estate** program initially called Hollywoodland. Hollywood's studios developed into a successful entertainment industry exporting its production abroad. Major European actors and directors even chose to settle in Hollywood where the real thing was.

Cinema

Other members of the Commonwealth are interesting examples of culture as a soft power.
Firstly, Nigeria has always been politically and culturally influential on the African continent thanks to its large population and enormous oil wealth. Nigeria's hugely popular film industry, Nollywood, is the country's second largest employer in a country with an economy that relies mainly on oil and agriculture. It also includes diaspora films i.e. movies shot in any non-African country but targeting the Nigerian audience. The term **mirrors** two of the most famous areas of film production: Hollywood in the United States, and Bollywood in India's Bombay, even if it doesn't generate the same **revenues**. While Nollywood is already well-established across the African continent, Nigerian movies are beginning to reach audiences in Europe and the United States, leading to an increased international consumption of Nigerian films.
Secondly, India has been a major transmitter of culture across Asia and beyond. Bollywood, India's flamboyant film industry, has contributed to its global presence and prestige.

Vocabulaire

Epitomizes illustrates
Has followed suit has done the same
Real estate property
Mirrors reflects
Revenues profits

Actualité

By undermining American commitment to longstanding international cooperation, Trump has diminished the United States' soft power. The Biden-Harris administration can reverse that tide. Even if Biden will always support US commercial interests, no doubt, he will prioritize multilateral cooperation in his efforts to deal with global challenges, leading to a revival in American soft power. Biden's communications style and leadership is what America and the world need to unite in response to the pandemic as well as the economic and climate crisis.

Exercices

01 Civilization

The Hollywood sign.

Right or Wrong?

1) Hollywood is located in San Francisco. ○ Right ○ Wrong

2) The Hollywood sign was initially a real estate sign. ○ Right ○ Wrong

3) The photograph conveys the idea of straight path to success. ○ Right ○ Wrong

4) Hollywood epitomizes the American worldwide influence. ○ Right ○ Wrong

5) The decolonization of the British Empire is a period that started with the independence of the United States. ○ Right ○ Wrong

6) Americanization is a soft power. ○ Right ○ Wrong

7) Nollywood is the name of the cinema industry in India. ○ Right ○ Wrong

8) Hollywood generates less profit than Nollywood. ○ Right ○ Wrong

9) Charlie Chaplin is an American actor and movie maker. ○ Right ○ Wrong

10) The City is the name of New York's financial district. ○ Right ○ Wrong

02 Vocabulary

A) Complete the text with the following words.

a) audience • b) culture • c) influence • d) diaspora • e) power • f) imperialism • g) film industry

I) Starting in the early 1990s, Nollywood has quickly exerted .... [1] and gained worldwide recognition as the world's second most prolific .... [2].

II) Watching Nollywood films was significant in increasing participants' knowledge and appreciation of .... [3].

III) Nollywood films are likely to lead to cross-cultural transmission of Nigeria's cultural heritage to audience as such as another form of .... [4].

IV) These films are typically made by Nigerian filmmakers living in the .... [5] and they are typically made for the Nigerian .... [6].

V) Today, Nollywood epitomizes Nigeria's soft .... [7] on the African continent.

B) Translate these sentences into English.

a) La mondialisation a été critiquée d'être une forme déguisée de l'hégémonie occidentale sur les pays en développement.

....

....

....

b) La forme de standardisation de la culture mondiale est appelée l'américanisation par certains.

....

....

....

c) Les pays anglo-saxons sont confrontés aujourd'hui au besoin de redéfinir leur rôle et d'affirmer leur force.

....

....

....

d) Les superpuissances sont forcées de remettre en question leur place dans un monde où le pouvoir non partagé est devenu illusoire.

....

....

Rivalries and interdependences

Rivalités et interdépendances

Trade

Nowadays, most nations are interdependent and related in a globalized world. Economic interdependence plays a major role in influencing the nature and content of inter-state relations. It lowers the possibility of international conflict by increasing the significance of trading: states trade rather than invade. Nonetheless, it does not completely prevent the **outbreak** of rivalries.
As China was becoming one of the world's fastest-growing economies, the relationship between China and the United States went from having no trade to a very significant level of economic interdependence. More recently, the United States decided to protect American jobs from unfair foreign competition. In that case, the increased protectionism from the United States can contribute to lead to more negative results for its trading partners.
The most comprehensive international organization for accelerating international cooperation and for the maintenance of international peace is the UN (United Nations) created after World War II.
On the global scale, the WTO (World Trade Organization) and the IMF (International Monetary Fund) facilitate international trade and financial stability between nations. Other examples of free-trade agreements range from the NAFTA (North American Free Trade Agreement) between Canada, Mexico and the United States, and the CETA (Comprehensive Economic and Trade Agreement) between Canada and the European Union.

Federalism

In the United States, the adoption of a federation at the **outset** of the nation's history reflected that the Founding Fathers were driven by a desire to **strike** a balance in power between a federal government and the several state governments. Surely the transformation from a collection of thirteen historically separated states clustered along the Atlantic coast to a group of fifty states largely spread on territory has played a role in the development of the federal system. As the relationships between the federal government and the states have evolved over time through constant negotiation, federalism has repeatedly proven to serve as a major asset.
On the contrary, federalism is also characterized by rivalry, whether it is the clashes between the federal power and the states or the competition among states.
Furthermore, individual states have economies that rival countries many times their size. For instance, California's economy is the largest of any state. Its closest comparison on a global stage is India. California's massive economy is **bolstered** by a diverse range of industries from agriculture to technology. California has the highest population in the United States and most Americans move to this state.

Vocabulaire

Outbreak eruption
Outset beginning
Strike reach
Bolstered supported

Liberalism

The world entered the coronavirus pandemic with persistent imbalances. The crisis has caused a sharp reduction in trade and new trade barriers are effective in reducing imbalances.
Liberalism is often said to be the blame for economic crisis. Economic liberalism obviously has virtues because it creates wealth, multiplies exchanges and inspires innovation. Free trade and capitalism are often **hallmarks** of economic liberalism. It also has limitations: it can lead to dominance and accommodate unemployment, poverty and inequality.
Capitalism has led to a massive increase in new technologies over the past decades. This technology improves productivity and has led to better paid jobs. As a case point, the GAFAM companies are the five most valuable companies. GAFAM is an acronym that refers to Google, Amazon, Facebook, Apple, and Microsoft, often blamed for monopolistic practices and privacy and free speech concerns.

Immigration

Free trade reduces barriers between nations and promotes global economic growth. **Labor** can move from country to country to market their skills. As a consequence, more and more countries are experiencing significant volumes of migrations. That is why mobility is a characteristic of today's world and implies an increasing number of connections, exchanges and partnerships. It recognizes the world as a complex web of interdependencies, where citizens' actions have repercussions for individuals and communities locally, nationally and internationally.
Commonwealth citizens hold an international status within the former British Empire. For those looking to immigrate to other Commonwealth nations, the immigration process may be easier. Canada and the United States have one of the highest immigration rates in the world. Thousands of individuals immigrate every year for many reasons. Recently, since the United Kingdom voted for Brexit, there has been an increase of people intending to move to Canada from the United Kingdom.
Families crossing the United States border without a visa demonstrating they are admissible to the country are subject to detention. Asylum seekers, migrants, children, families **Fleeing** violence, abuse and poverty are **detained** in overcrowded detention facilities.

Vocabulaire

Hallmarks characteristics
Labor workforce
Fleeing escaping from
Detained incarcerated

Actualité

Since the first day of the Biden administration, the President has begun to reshape the nation's immigration policy, which he considers a moral imperative. He pledges to limit the construction of the border wall and to better provide safe processing of asylum seekers at the border. Reuniting the families is one of the Biden administration's top priorities. During former President Trump's time in office, thousands of migrant children were separated from their parents when they entered the country. The Biden administration will allow them to reunite with their families in the United States, and some families may have the opportunity to stay.

Exercices

01 Reading

DETAINED–HOW THE UNITED STATES BUILT THE WORLD'S LARGEST IMMIGRANT DETENTION SYSTEM

Children sleeping on floors, changing other children's diapers. Families torn apart at the .... [1]. .... [2] crammed into fetid .... [3] centers. These have become familiar sights as people fleeing gang .... [4], domestic abuse and .... [5] arrive on the southern border of the United States. Many will join more than 52,000 immigrants confined in jails, prisons, tents and other forms of detention – most of them for profit.

The United States' reliance on immigrant detention is not a new phenomenon, nor did it emerge with Donald Trump.

The people held in prison-like facilities across the country are not **serving time** for a crime. They're waiting for a **hearing** to determine whether they can legally remain in the country.

Immigrants, including .... [6] and legal migrants, wait an average of more than four weeks to be released, though some have been held inside for years or even decades. Up to 2,500 are children and parents fleeing war and violence in their home countries. Thousands have alleged sexual and physical abuse inside the facilities. Forty years ago, this system did not exist.

A modest system holding fewer than 3,000 migrants a day at the end of the 1970s, detention has now **morphed** into a **sprawling** machinery **ensnaring** immigrants across the country. And facilities operated under both Immigration and Customs Enforcement (ICE) and the border patrol continue to come under fire for holding people in squalid conditions with minimal access to .... [7] and medical care.

As the race for the 2020 presidential election heats up, Democratic candidates have **clamored** to **decry** Trump's immigration .... [8]. Nearly all candidates support an end to detention for asylum-seeking families. In the meantime Trump continues to redirect **funding** from other agencies to a detention system whose daily population has grown by more than 40% since he took office. And it's only getting bigger.

Adapted from Emily Kassie, theguardian.com, 24 Septembre 2019
Source: https://www.theguardian.com/us-news/2019/sep/24/detained-us-largest-immigrant-detention-trump

Exercices

A) Complete the text with the following words.

- a) hygiene
- b) migrants
- c) poverty
- d) border
- e) detention
- f) policies
- g) violence
- h) asylum seekers

Wordbox

- **Serving time** in prison
- **Hearing** audience
- **Morphed** changed
- **Sprawling** spreading
- **Ensnaring** trapping
- **Clamored** claimed
- **Decry** denounce
- **Funding** financing

B) Right or wrong?

1) In the detention centers, families are separated. ○ Right ○ Wrong
2) Immigrants are packed into detention facilities. ○ Right ○ Wrong
3) Immigrants are escaping from difficult situations in their home country. ○ Right ○ Wrong
4) The detention centers are unprofitable. ○ Right ○ Wrong
5) Immigrants are incarcerated because of a crime they perpetrated. ○ Right ○ Wrong
6) Detainees don't have access to hygiene and health care. ○ Right ○ Wrong

02 Vocabulary

Match the word with its contrary.

1 federal ○	○ rivalry a
2 crisis ○	○ wealth b
3 cooperation ○	○ stability c
4 capitalism ○	○ fairness d
5 inequality ○	○ central e
6 poverty ○	○ socialism f

Common heritage and diversity

Héritage commun et diversité

Unity in diversity

All countries in the world have their own cultural heritage and identity; these can mean factors like their religious beliefs, traditions and language. As opposed to uniformity, diversity particularly applies to English-speaking countries. Ethnic groups have their own culture and have a feeling of belonging together. It is this difference that can be said to provide cultural plurality to a country. Nations where there is much cultural diversity can also sometimes be known as a multicultural society.

A country is multicultural due to the immigration that has taken place there. In these circumstances it has been the responsibility of successive governments to promote policies that encourage unity, social cohesion and inclusion, to fight discrimination and inequality for all its citizens. Having diverse **peoples** and cultural heritages won't make a difference on condition that these people are valued, respected, welcomed and included. Diversity requires to cultivate a uniquely diverse environment that includes every group's heritage.

Canada's experience with plurality distinguishes it from most other countries. It is one of the most culturally diverse population in the world and immigrants are **drawn** by its quality of life and its reputation as an open society that welcomes newcomers and values diversity.

Multicultural heritage

English-speaking countries are becoming more and more **cosmopolitan**, where languages play an outstanding role for social integration and cohesion. Interestingly, whereas English is the predominent language in countries such as Australia, the United States, New Zealand, it is used as a **vehicular language** in India, Pakistan, and some other African countries.

The 20th century has witnessed the transformation of the United States from a predominately white population **rooted** in Western culture to a society with a variety of ethnic minorities. Hispanics, African and Asian Americans, American Indians, Alaska Natives, and Pacific Islanders together will make up close to half of the population. It is to create a new multiracial heritage in the United States, as a natural continuation of the salad bowl tradition, even though some view the rapid increase in ethnic minorities as a loss of America's European heritage.

Vocabulaire

- **Peoples** populations
- **Drawn** attracted
- **Cosmopolitan** multicultural
- **Vehicular language** language used between groups with different native languages
- **Rooted** attached

Maori heritage

As a source of identity, heritage is a valuable factor for empowering local communities and enabling vulnerable groups to participate fully in social and cultural life.

As an instance, Maori culture is a big part of New Zealand's identity: respecting, preserving and promoting diversity is vital for the nation. Maori culture has been passed on from generation to generation through art, music, storytelling and reciting genealogies. Maori heritage is **threefold**.

First of all, its natural asset such as mountains, volcanoes, geysers, springs, falls and reserves. They also have **carvings** which are inherited from the past and transmitted to future generations.

Secondly, its physical heritage is also extremely rich; it includes burial sites, archeological sites, artifacts, architectural styles, museums, libraries and archive collections.

Thirdly, cultural preservation and protection is a major concern for indigenous peoples who have become minorities in their own lands. Maori, the indigenous people, came to the island more than 1 000 years ago from their mythical Polynesian homeland of Hawaiki. Maori customs are to be known to be able to interact in Maori culture. The community maintains the mythology, traditions and rituals from the past: singing, dancing and tatooing are alive and well in New Zealand. Ferocious Maori war dances called haka are a must-see for any visitor and are the **trademark** of their worldwide famous rugby team the All Blacks.

Sports

Sports often feature patriotic rituals such as singing the national anthem. We can see that common heritage may be subject to acculturation, as in sports for instance.

Baseball and the other modern **bat**-and-ball games were developed from **folk** games in early Britain. English colonists took this game to America with their other pastimes, and variants were being played on both sides of the ocean under many appellations. Today, baseball and softball are mostly played in the United States and cricket and **rounders** in the United Kingdom.

Originated from soccer (football in British English), the game of rugby continued to develop and take root in many different countries, largely thanks to Britain's imperial **endeavors**. In the United States, (American) football is the most popular sport, followed by baseball, basketball, and ice hockey. (American) football resulted from several major associations between soccer and rugby. In Australia, the legacy continues with Australian football.

Vocabulaire

- **Threefold** in three parts
- **Carvings** sculptures
- **Trademark** distinctive characteristic
- **Bat** a type of racket
- **Folk** popular
- **Rounders** a type a baseball
- **Endeavors** efforts

Actualité

The Olympic Games has always been subject to rivalry. It is a way to show a country's power, measuring the performance of its sportsmen. During the games, unity prevails and countries come together. People get the chance to see their country strive for glory. As a matter of fact, the United States is the most prolific medal-winning nation in the history of the Olympics, and, obviously, cultural pride permeates this event. It should come as no surprise that hosting the event has an impact on national image as well.

Exercices

01 Civilization

Watch this video and answer the questions.

Title : On bended knee; Kaepernick sits for anthem again, surrounded by military

https://www.youtube.com/watch?v=75qnEiOrHlI&ab_channel=CBSLosAngeles

1) Where is the stadium located?
- ☐ **a.** In San Diego
- ☐ **b.** In San Francisco

2) What is Colin Kaepernick's job?
- ☐ **a.** He is a professional soccer player
- ☐ **b.** He is a professional football player

3) What is Colin Kaepernick's position in the team?
- ☐ **a.** Quarterback
- ☐ **b.** Running back

4) What is the name of his team?
- ☐ **a.** The 49ers
- ☐ **b.** Seahawks

5) What was he reluctant to do?
- ☐ **a.** To stand during the national anthem
- ☐ **b.** To kneel

6) What does Colin Kaepernick want to denounce?
- ☐ **a.** Injustices toward people of color
- ☐ **b.** Military forces

7) What do people think?
- ☐ **a.** That he has the right not to stand for the anthem
- ☐ **b.** That he has to stand for the anthem

8) Another player refused to stand, where?
- ☐ **a.** Seattle
- ☐ **b.** Oakland

9) What is the first origin of American football?
- ☐ **a.** Soccer
- ☐ **b.** Rugby

10) Where is softball mostly played?
- ☐ **a.** In the United Kingdom
- ☐ **b.** In the United States

02 Vocabulary

Fill in the crossword.

Horizontal
3) member of a country
4) speech
5) native
6) hymn
7) legacy
8) integration
9) age groups
10) cosmopolitan
11) multiculturalism
12) cohesion

Vertical
1) customs
2) protection
6) assimilation to a culture
10) legends

Synthesis: Power and influence

Imperialism

- Power and influence are at the heart of international relations
- The British Empire: from domination to decolonization
- American hegemony as a superpower but in decline

The BBC

- The BBC is the world's oldest national broadcaster
- High reputation and a global brand
- Its prominent role in British worldwide influence

Power and influence

Global village

- American soft power: films and music and the American lifestyle
- The American non-territorial influence known as globalization
- Hollywood's influence on the global village

Cinema

- Nigeria's soft power: Nollywood, including diaspora films
- Nollywood's influence on the African continent and emergence on the world stage
- India's soft power: Bollywood

Synthesis: Rivalries and interdependences

Rivalries and interdependences

Trade

- Nations are interdependent: less rivalry and more trade
- The relation between China and the United States: from no trade to interdependence
- Many institutions support international cooperation: the UN, the WTO, the IMF, the NAFTA, the CETA

Federalism

- The United States: a federation of 50 states
- Federalism also means rivalry between the federations and competition between states
- California: the largest economy

Liberalism

- Liberalism as a cause for the economic crisis
- The upsides of liberalism
- Capitalism and the GAFAM

Immigration

- The global economic growth fosters mobility
- Commonwealth citizens' status to facilitate mobility
- Canada and the United States: high immigration rate countries
- In the United States, immigrants in detention centers

Synthesis: Common heritage and diversity

Unity in diversity

- English-speaking countries have their own cultural heritage and diversity
- Immigration makes a country multicultural
- Canada's experience one of the most culturally diverse population

Multicultural heritage

- English-speaking countries are cosmopolitan
- English is either a predominent language or a vehicular language
- The United States is getting more diverse following the trend of the Salad bowl

Common heritage and diversity

Maori heritage

- Maori culture is part of New Zealand's identity
- The heritage of the island is natural, physical and cultural
- The All Blacks are famous worldwide

Sports

- Common heritage and acculturation in sports
- From British origin, baseball and softball in the United States, cricket and rounders in the United Kingdom
- Different forms of soccer, rugby, and football according to the country

Corrigés

Knowledge, creation, innovation

Production and circulation of knowledge

● Production et circulation des savoirs

Reading .... p. 10

A) Complete the text with the following words.

1) **f.** position • 2) **b.** information • 3) **k.** universities • 4) **a.** vote • 5) **e.** brain-drain • 6) **i.** research • 7) **g.** talented • 8) **h.** academics • 9) **c.** competitive • 10) **j.** colleagues • 11) **d.** unwelcome

B) Put the main ideas of the text in the right order.

1) **f.** 11,000 academics left between 2016 and 2019.
2) **a.** Academics even left the highest-ranked universities.
3) **e.** The Liberal Democrats are worried about the brain drain caused by Brexit.
4) **b.** Academics are concerned about their status and the research funding.
5) **d.** The European Union research funding for the United Kingdom is decreasing.
6) **c.** The Conservative Party is inflicting contentious issues following Brexit.

Vocabulary .... p. 11

Match the following words with the correct definition.

1) Knowledge ▸ **h.** information and skills acquired through experience or education • 2) Innovation ▸ **f.** the action or process of innovating • 3) University ▸ **e.** a high-level educational institution • 4) Dissemination ▸ **i.** the action or fact of spreading something (especially information) widely • 5) Heritage ▸ **d.** valued things or traditions passed down from previous generations • 6) Digital divide ▸ **b.** the gap between those who have access to computers and those who do not • 7) Self-taught ▸ **a.** to be autodidact • 8) Digital learning ▸ **g.** education using technology • 9) Collaboration ▸ **c.** teamwork

Sciences and technologies, promises and challenges

● Sciences et techniques, promesses et défis

Civilization .... p. 14

1) **a.** 100 million
2) **b.** In 190 countries
3) **b.** Mail order DVD service
4) **a.** Internet video on demand
5) **a.** Watching an entire season in one go
6) **a.** Improvement in streaming technology and rise of handled devices
7) **b.** Produce their own online-only television series
8) **a.** 126
9) **a.** Double original programming
10) **b.** Live TV

Vocabulary .... p. 15

Understanding .... p. 16

A) Answer the questions about sciences and technologies.

1) The United States is the leader in the race to innovation.

2) The space industry and smartphone industry have been steadily growing.

3) Canada, the United Kingdom, Jamaica, Nigeria are intending to foster innovation.

4) Transhumanism is the development of the human condition with technology.

5) AI can boost competitiveness and productivity, help reduce errors, make decisions more easily and carry out actions more rapidly.

6) Co-working allows to become more adaptable and collaborative, empowering a more independent and entrepreneurial workforce.

7) Employees commute less and use their time more efficiently. It participates in the improvement of the family well-being and in reducing the environmental footprint.

8) The film industry has changed with the emergence of technologies such as the autonomous drones, 3D, computer animation and streaming.

B) Match the two parts of the sentences.

1) **f.** Organize your workspace without distractions to be able to concentrate.

2) **b.** Use ergonomic work furniture to maintain a comfortable and neutral body posture

3) **d.** Secure your Internet connection to access corporate data safely.

4) **c.** Give yourself a fixed schedule to structure your days including your breaks.

5) **e.** Set daily goals and tasks to be able to track your work progress.

6) **a.** Optimize communication with the team to collaborate effectively.

Representations

Make one's voice heard: representation and participation

● Faire entendre sa voix : représentation et participation

Civilization .... p. 22

1) **a.** He is an activist calling on pedestrians to join a protest
2) **b.** A revolutionary South African leader
3) **a.** The Anti-Apartheid Revolution
4) **a.** China
5) **a.** 1997
6) **b.** A series of protests
7) **b.** To protest regarding an amendment bill hindering Hong Kong's autonomy
8) **a.** The Republic of Ireland
9) **b.** A president
10) **b.** 54

Vocabulary .... p. 23

A) Complete the sentences with the following words.

I) **c.** parties • **f.** democrats
II) **i.** candidate • **h.** campaign
III) **a.** vice-president • **d.** voters
IV) **b.** referendums • **g.** legislation
V) **e.** presidential • **j.** landslide

B) Translate these sentences into English.

a) It is well-known that the monarchy is the oldest institution in Great Britain and is the symbol of British identity.
b) The monarchy echoes the idea of tradition and embodies the hopes and beliefs of the British people.
c) Public debates have divided the nation into two groups: the monarchists and the republicans.
d) The predicaments suffered by the Windsor family are considered as a crisis resulting from the clash between traditions and modernism.
e) The British monarch is determined to protect their political neutrality to represent the whole country.

C) Match the word with its definition.

1) Referendum ▸ **c.** A general vote by the electorate on a single political question.
2) Devolution ▸ **g.** The transfer of power from the central government to regional administration.
3) Westminster ▸ **a.** The site of the British Houses of Parliament.
4) Éire ▸ **f.** The Irish name for Ireland.
5) Dominion ▸ **d.** The territory of a sovereign government.
6) Constitution ▸ **b.** A text of fundamental principles according to which a state is governed.
7) Commonwealth ▸ **e.** An association of countries that were previously part of the British Empire.

Inform and get informed

● Informer et s'informer

Civilization .... p. 26

A) Complete the text with the following words.

1) **c.** outlets
2) **b.** trusted
3) **f.** anonymous
4) **j.** story
5) **i.** editorial
6) **d.** resignations
7) **a.** journalists
8) **e.** fake news
9) **g.** sources
10) **h.** narrative

B) Put the main ideas of the text in the right order.

1) **d.** The accusations of fake news of the president undermining news outlets professionalism
2) **c.** CNN denounced a connection between a Russian investor and the president's ally Scaramucci
3) **e.** CNN apologized for the journalists' lack of fact-checking
4) **b.** Unlike Scaramucci, the president kept on making a fuss about the story
5) **a.** The president uses fake news for its political narrative

C) What is the author's point of view? Answer these questions.

1) **b.** Wrong • 2) **a.** Right • 3) **b.** Wrong • 4) **a.** Right • 5) **b.** Wrong

Represent the world and represent oneself

● Représenter le monde et se représenter

Civilization .... p. 30

1) **a.** bushfires
2) **b.** Smog
3) **b.** Fires that are up two hundred kilometers away
4) **a.** helplessness
5) **b.** Bushfires have taken the lives of thousands of koalas
6) **a.** With a drone
7) **a.** verbalize his emotions
8) **b.** Anonymity
9) **b.** To pay tribute
10) **a.** Drought

Vocabulary .... p. 31

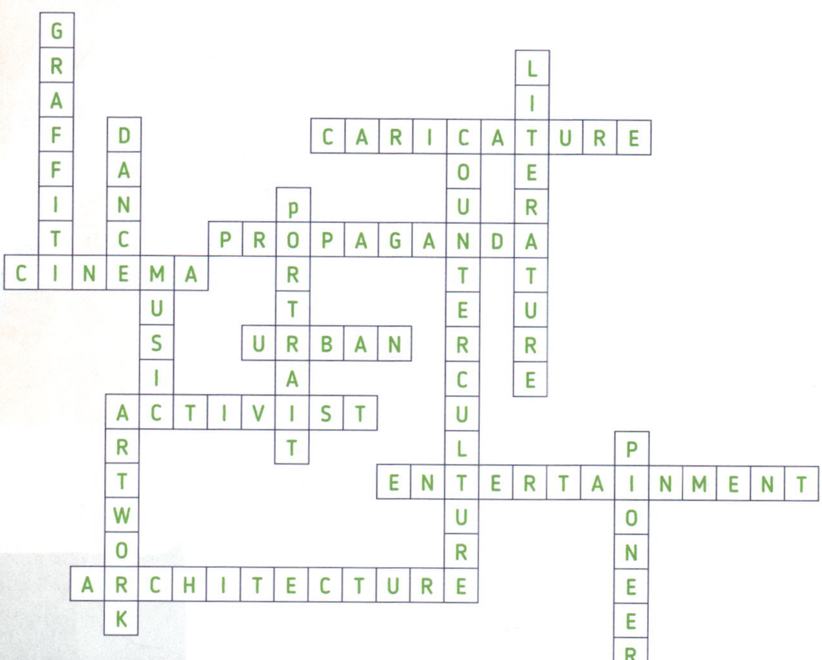

Be a society

Unity and plurality

● Unité et pluralité

Civilization .... p. 38

1) **b.** The United States of America
2) **a.** John F. Kennedy
3) **a.** The nation was built with several waves of immigration
4) **b.** Ellis island
5) **b.** Emma Lazarus
6) **a.** A society which assimilates immigrants
7) **a.** Barack Obama
8) **a.** A multicultural society
9) **b.** It is declining
10) **b.** California, Florida, Texas

Vocabulary .... p. 39

A) Complete the text with the following words.

1) **j.** white
2) **i.** culture
3) **d.** ethnic
4) **e.** minority
5) **b.** population
6) **c.** multiracial
7) **f.** melting-pot
8) **a.** heritage
9) **g.** income
10) **h.** education

B) Translate these sentences into English.

a) Plurality represents the full range of human differences such as ethnicity, religion, gender, sexual orientation, age, socio-economic status or disability.

b) Diversity also features a variety in personalities, lifestyles, opinions, family composition, or education level.

c) Unity refers to a feeling of belonging and implies to cultivate an inclusive environment.

d) Societies are becoming more and more multicultural and cosmopolitan.

e) An inclusive society aims at promoting the social, economic, and political integration of all.

Public liberties and individual liberties

● Libertés publiques et libertés individuelles

Reading .... p. 42

A) Complete the text with the following words.

1) **f.** First Nations
2) **a.** policies
3) **g.** legacy
4) **d.** communities
5) **h.** assimilation
6) **b.** descendants
7) **e.** removals
8) **c.** compensation

B) Put the main ideas of the text in the right order.

1) **b.** The generations of children removed from their families are called the Stolen generations.
2) **a.** The principle of the policy.
3) **d.** The assimilation of children.
4) **e.** The impacts of the policy.
5) **c.** The compensation.

Civilization .... p. 43

Match the word with the definition.

1) The American Dream ▸ **b.** The belief that every American can be successful with hard work.
2) The First amendment ▸ **c.** The element of the Constitution that guarantees Free Speech.
3) The War of independence ▸ **f.** The revolutionary war of the 13 colonies and Britain.
4) The Pilgrim Fathers ▸ **h.** The first settlers.
5) The Founding Fathers ▸ **e.** The originators of the Constitution.
6) Rag to riches ▸ **a.** Upward social mobility.
7) A self-made man ▸ **j.** An independently successful man.
8) The Cold War ▸ **d.** The period of political tensions between the Soviet Union and the USA.
9) Rockefeller ▸ **g.** A famous rich businessman.
10) Puritan ▸ **i.** Someone who believes in hard work, in the protestant tradition.

Equalities and inequalities

● Égalités et inégalités

Civilization .... p. 46

1) **b.** A trailer
2) **a.** London
3) **b.** At separate tables
4) **b.** 165 Eaton Place
5) **b.** World War II
6) **a.** He is one of the servants
7) **a.** Indians served in the army to fight for the British
8) **a.** It talks about social class
9) **b.** To rise to a higher social position.
10) **a.** An association of the best universities in the United Kingdom.

Vocabulary .... p. 47

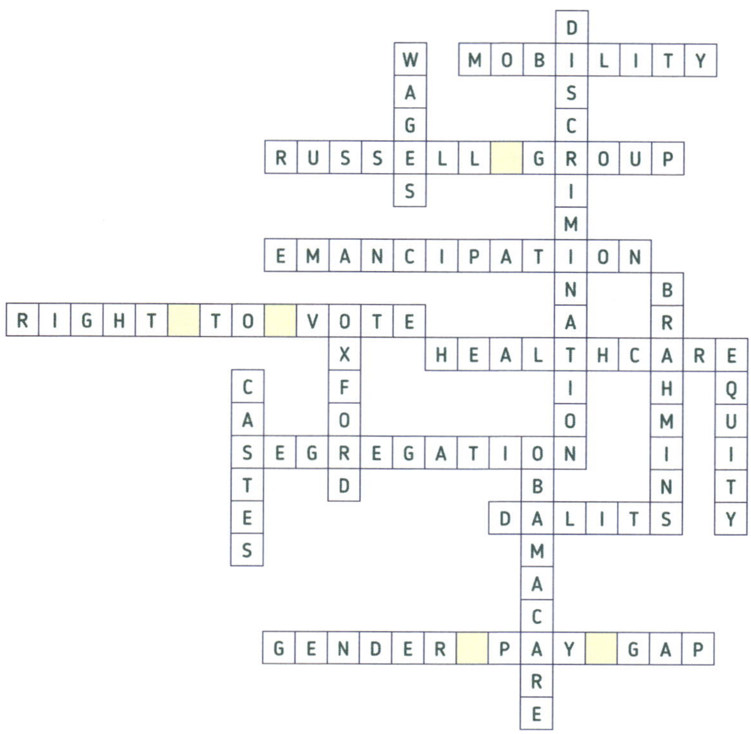

Changing environments

Frontier and space

● Frontière et espace

Civilization .... p. 54

1) Right
2) Wrong. The picture conveys the idea of length.
3) Wrong. The US-Mexican border is 2,000 miles long.
4) Right
5) Right
6) Right
7) Wrong. Detroit and Chicago are situated in the Rust Belt.
8) Right
9) Wrong. The Founding Fathers are the leaders of the war of independence (1775-1783).
10) Right

Culture .... p. 55

1) **c.** • 2) **b.** • 3) **d.** • 4) **a.** • 5) **j.** • 6) **h.** • 7) **i.** • 8) **g.** • 9) **f.** • 10) **e.**

Language .... p. 56

a) Digital technologies have deeply transformed the relationship between individuals.
b) Since the rise of social media, remaining in contact with relatives has become effortless.
c) Today, you can publish information and communicate using several devices.
d) One of the obvious upsides of social networks is that you can instantly reach people from anywhere.
e) The Internet has contributed to bridge the digital divide by giving access to information and knowledge.

From the protection of nature to ecological transition

● De la protection de la nature à la transition écologique

Reading .... p. 58

Complete the text with the following words.

1) **a.** monsoon • 2) **d.** land • 3) **c.** rains • 4) **b.** desert • 5) **f.** floods • 6) **e.** shortage • 7) **i.** crops • 8) **h.** landslides • 9) **g.** earthquakes • 10) **j.** foothills

Vocabulary .... p. 59

A) Complete the map with the main territories.

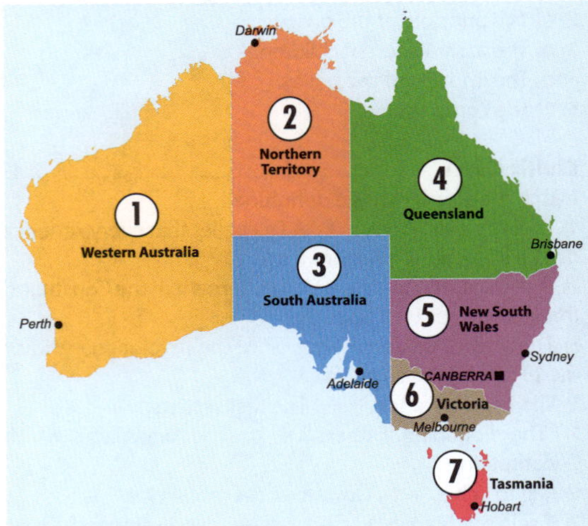

B) Associate two words to create a compound noun.

1) fossil ▸ fuels
2) natural ▸ resources
3) bush ▸ fires
4) climate ▸ change
5) land ▸ preservation
6) oil ▸ drilling
7) food ▸ shortage
8) heat ▸ waves
9) global ▸ warming
10) greenhouse ▸ gases

Rethink the city

● Repenser la ville

Civilization .... p. 62

1) **a.** The message is to inform about the issue of global cities
2) **b.** Nearly 1 billion people reside in 60 Global cities
3) **a.** Global cities are economic powerhouses
4) **a.** Infrastructures
5) **a.** A monument in Chicago
6) **b.** Knowledge
7) **a.** Culture
8) **a.** Politics
9) **b.** It means to understand the importance of connecting local politics to global politics
10) **a.** Openness

Language .... p. 63

A) Separate the words with a dash

Diversity - urban - population - city - slums - countries - megalopolis - startups - gentrification - ghetto - township

B) Classify the words in two columns: adjectives and nouns

Adjectives	Nouns
spatial	development
distinct	areas
urban	inequalities
gated	deprivation
impoverished	communities
segregated	cohesion
social	apartheid
underdeveloped	

C) Find as many words as you can by matching the two parts.

1) Considerable
2) Worker • Workless
3) Powerful • powerless • powerness
4) Countless • countable
5) Business • busier
6) Mostly
7) Neighborhood

Relation with the world

Power and influence

● Puissance et influence

Civilization .... p. 70

1) Wrong. Hollywood is located in Los Angeles.
2) Right
3) Right
4) Right
5) Wrong. The decolonization of the British Empire is a period that started with the independence of India.
6) Right
7) Wrong. Bollywood is the name of the cinema industry in India.
8) Wrong. Hollywood generates more profit than Nollywood.
9) Right
10) Wrong. Wall Street is the name of New York's financial district.

Vocabulary .... p. 71

A) Complete the text with the following words.

I) **c.** influence • **g.** film industry
II) **b.** culture
III) **f.** imperialism
IV) **d.** diaspora • **a.** audience
V) **e.** power

B) Translate these sentences into English.

a) Globalization has been blamed for being a disguised form of western hegemony over developing countries.
b) The form of standardization of culture worldwide is called Americanization by some.
c) English-speaking countries are faced today with the need to redefine their role and assert their strength.
d) Superpowers are forced to question their place in a world where unshared power has become illusory.

Rivalries and interdependences

● Rivalités et interdépendances

Reading .... p. 74

A) Complete the text with the following words.

1) **d.** border
2) **b.** migrants
3) **e.** detention
4) **g.** violence
5) **c.** poverty
6) **h.** asylum seekers
7) **a.** hygiene
8) **f.** policies

B) Right or Wrong?

1) Right
2) Right
3) Right
4) Wrong. The detention centers are built for profit.
5) Wrong. Immigrants are incarcerated because they are waiting for a hearing, they are not serving time for a crime.
6) Right

Vocabulary .... p. 75

1) federal ▸ **e.** central
2) crisis ▸ **c.** stability
3) cooperation ▸ **a.** rivalry
4) capitalism ▸ **f.** socialism
5) inequality ▸ **d.** fairness
6) poverty ▸ **b.** wealth

Common heritage and diversity

● Héritage commun et diversité

Civilization .... p. 78

1) **a.** In San Diego
2) **b.** He is a professional football player
3) **a.** Quarterback
4) **a.** The 49ers
5) **a.** To stand during the national anthem
6) **a.** Injustices toward people of color
7) **a.** That he has the right not to stand for the anthem
8) **b.** Oakland
9) **a.** Soccer
10) **b.** In the United States

Vocabulary .... p. 79

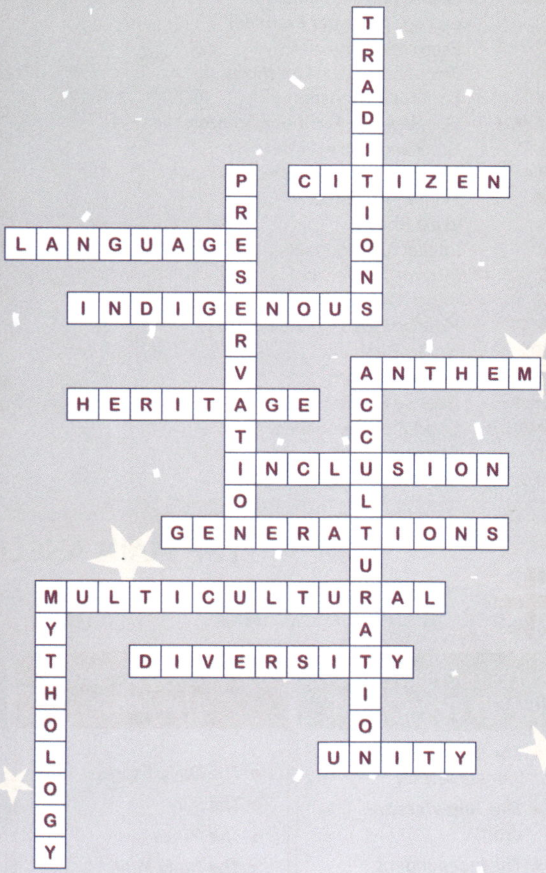

ANNEXES

ABBREVIATIONS AND ACRONYMS

AI	Artificial Intelligence
AIDS	Acquired ImmunoDeficiency Syndrome
AKA	Also Known As (alias)
AM/PM	Ante Meridiem (morning) / Post Meridiem (afternoon)
ASAP	As Soon As Possible
B.A.	Bachelor of Art
BBC	British Broadcasting Corporation
BC / AD	Before Christ / Anno Domini (after Christ)
BREXIT	British exit
BTW	By The Way
CC/BCC	Carbon Copy/Blind Carbon Copy
COVID	Coronavirus disease
DIY	Do It Yourself
DOB	Date Of Birth
DNA	Desoxyribo-Nucleic Acid
e.g.	exampli gratia (for example)
ETA	Estimated Time of Arrival
FAQ	Frequently Asked Questions
FYI	For Your Information
GAFAM	Google Apple Facebook Amazon Microsoft
GMT	Greenwich Mean Time
HIV	Human Immunodeficiency Viruses
HR	Human Resources
i.e.	id est (that is)
IQ	Intellectual Quotient
IT	Information Technology
KO	Knock Out
MOOCs	Massive Open Online Courses
NBD	No Big Deal
PR	Public Relations
Sci-Fi	Science Fiction
SMS	Short Message Service
St.	Street
UFO	Unidentified Flying Object
UK	United Kingdom
US/USA	United States of America
VAT	Value Added Tax
WASP	White Anglo-Saxon Protestant
WWI	World War I
WWII	World War II
WWW	World Wide Web
X-ing	Crossing
Xmas	Christmas

Institutions

CETA	Comprehensive Economic and Trade Agreement
COP	Conferences Of the Parties
EAEC/ EURATOM	European Atomic Energy Community
EEC	European Economic Community
ECB	European Central Bank
EU	European Union
FAO	Food and Agriculture Organization of the United Nations
GATT	General Agreement on Tariffs and Trade
ICE	Immigration and Customs Enforcement
IMF	International Monetary Fund
MIT	Massachussets Institute of Technology
NATFA	North American Free Trade Agreement
NATO	North Atlantic Treaty Organization
NGO	Non-Governmental Organization
UNESCO	United Nations Educational, Scientific and Cultural Organization
UNICEF	United Nations International Children's Emergency Fund
UN	United Nations Organization
WHO	World Health Organization
WTO	World Trade Organization
WWF	World Wide Fund for Nature

THE MAIN ANGLOPHONE MEDIA

Les médias britanniques

LES QUOTIDIENS DE QUALITÉ (BROADSHEETS)

- *The Daily Telegraph* (conservateur)
- *The Times* (centre droit)
- *The Independent* (centre gauche)
- *The Guardian* (gauche)
- *The Observer* (gauche)

LA PRESSE À SENSATION (TABLOÏDS)

- *The Daily Express*
- *The Sun*
- *The Mirror*
- *The Daily Mail*
- *The Evening Standard* (Londres)

LES HEBDOMADAIRES

- *The Financial Times*
- *The Economist*
- *The New Statesman*
- *The New Scientist*

TÉLÉVISION/RADIO

- BBC
- Sky News
- ITV
- Channel 4

Les médias américains

LES QUOTIDIENS

- *The Washington Post*
- *The New York Times*
- *The International Herald Tribune*
- *The Los Angeles Times*
- *The Wall Street Journal*
- *USA Today*

LES HEBDOMADAIRES

- *Time Magazine*
- *Newsweek*
- *Business Week*

TÉLÉVISION/RADIO

- CNN
- NBC
- CBS
- NPR
- Fox News
- ABC

THE COMMONWEALTH OF NATIONS

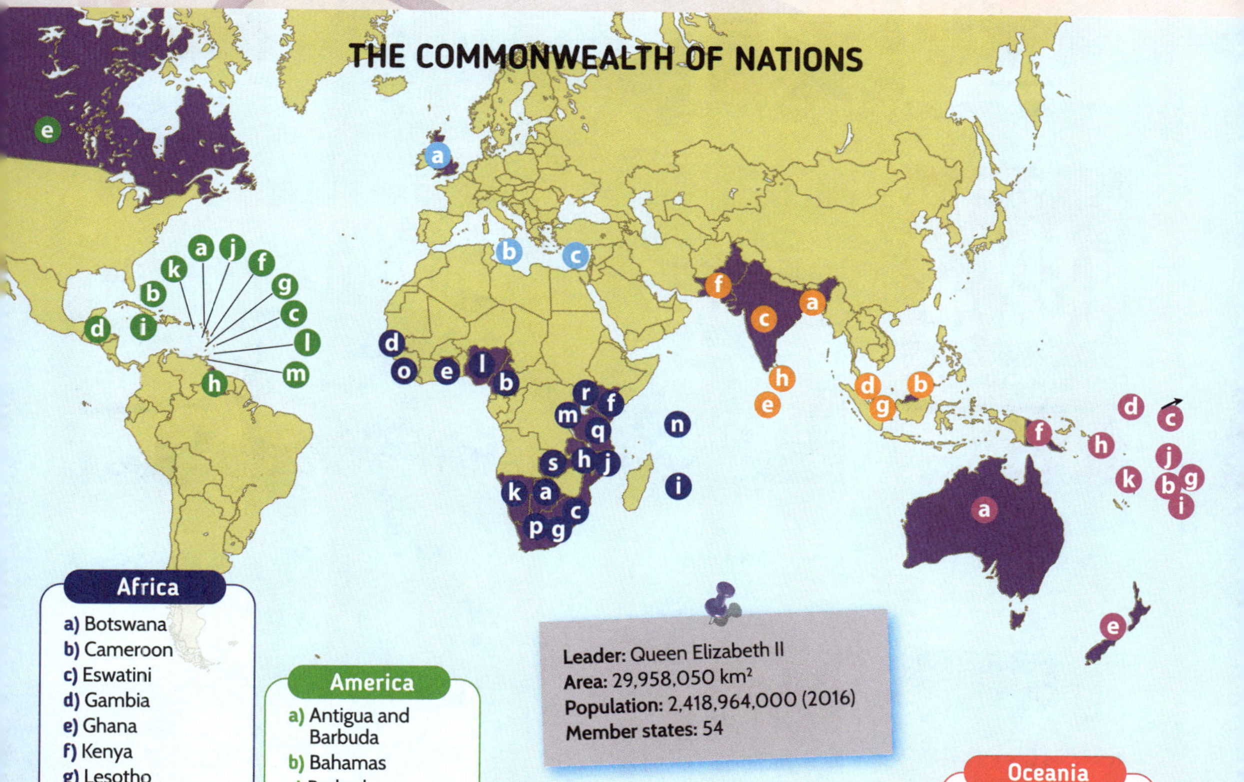

Leader: Queen Elizabeth II
Area: 29,958,050 km^2
Population: 2,418,964,000 (2016)
Member states: 54

Africa

a) Botswana
b) Cameroon
c) Eswatini
d) Gambia
e) Ghana
f) Kenya
g) Lesotho
h) Malawi
i) Mauritius
j) Mozambique
k) Namibia
l) Nigeria
m) Rwanda
n) Seychelles
o) Sierra Leone
p) South Africa
q) Tanzania
r) Uganda
s) Zambia

America

a) Antigua and Barbuda
b) Bahamas
c) Barbados
d) Belize
e) Canada
f) Dominica
g) Grenada
h) Guyana
i) Jamaica
j) Saint Lucia
k) St Kitts and Nevis
l) St Vincent and The Grenadines
m) Trinidad and Tobago

Asia

a) Bangladesh
b) Brunei
c) India
d) Malaysia
e) Maldives
f) Pakistan
g) Singapore
h) Sri Lanka

Europe

a) United Kingdom
b) Malta
c) Cyprus

Oceania

a) Australia
b) Fiji
c) Kiribati
d) Nauru
e) New Zealand
f) Papua New Guinea
g) Samoa
h) Solomon Islands
i) Tonga
j) Tuvalu
k) Vanuatu

Retrouvez nos ouvrages

Commandez-les sur le site
librairie.studyrama.com

Studyrama

Composition : **Stéphane Mac Donald**
Édition : **Benjamin Dias Pereira,** assisté de **Laureen Gatien**
Imprimé en France en 2021 : par Evoluprint - 31150 Bruguières
ISBN : 978-2-7590-4678-2